Desperate Measures

Book Three
In the Desperate Horse Wives Trilogy

Janet R Fox

ISBN-10:1982022043
ISBN-13: 978-1982022044

Happy trails to you!
Janet R Fox

DEDICATION

To Jack, To Dave

CONTENTS

Chapter One

Desperate Horse Wives

Four riders pulled their horses up to grab the rain gear tied on the backs of their saddles. The horses stood steady as the women turned in their saddles, untied the bundles, and swung their coats around themselves putting them on. These were well-trained, well-mannered trail horses accustomed to many things that would unsettle less experienced horses.

The women had not expected rain. When they left home Friday for this horse camping trip on an October holiday weekend, the prediction was only for ten percent chance of rain on Monday, Columbus Day. They always carried rain coats, flashlights, water, food, lead ropes, hoof picks, vet wrap, lunches, and cell phones as they rode trail.

"Everyone ready?" Nancy Reynolds asked as she looked around at her group of friends. They had been riding together on monthly camping trips and as many day rides as they could schedule for the last three and a half years. She was the oldest at seventy. Under her riding helmet was short, light brown hair streaked with plenty of gray. She was wearing a short, Australian, out-back oil slicker.

"Wait a sec', I still have to put my helmet cover on." Jolene Parker, the youngest in the group at seventeen, unfolded a plastic rain cover and slipped it over her riding helmet. Her long, blond ponytail hung down her back, unprotected from the rain. She stuffed it under her blue, plastic, rain coat although it was already drenched. Her long legs clad in blue jeans were soaked. "OK, I'm ready."

Nancy turned her horse, Bright Beauty, to head down the trail in the direction they had been traveling. Beauty was a Missouri Fox Trotter mare, a golden palomino with flaxen mane and tail that now hung wet and limp in the sudden rain storm.

When the trail widened, Jolene urged her black Tennessee Walker, Tricked Out, to catch up with her mother's horse, Tucker, another black Walker. "Mom, can you believe this rain? How much farther is it back to camp?"

"I don't know, Honey, but I hope it's close. It's raining harder, and I can barely see." Elise Parker squinted her eyes nearly shut in an attempt to keep the rain out. The visor on her helmet helped some. Her Australian oil slicker was the long style, but the rain found its way into the tops of her boots anyway. Elise was barely thirty-four. She gave birth to Jolene shortly after turning seventeen.

Tricked Out dropped back behind Tucker when the trail narrowed again. The dirt path was becoming muddy in the lower areas.

Trick put his head into Tucker's tail, trying to avoid the rain. His barn buddy, Tucker, allowed him to be there and did not kick him. Normally, Jolene would not allow them to travel so close, but she felt more secure being near enough to see the horse in front. The rain was driving harder and there was little else she could see through the gray sheets.

The fourth rider, bringing up the rear, was twenty-six-year-old Lavern Esser. She had taken back her maiden name after a divorce from Charlie Smith. She was riding her Tennessee Walker mare, Lacy, a rich brown with black mane, tail, and stockings. She called out to the group, "Hey, guys! Let's stop. I can't see a thing."

Nancy, in the lead, did not hear Lavern. Jolene called to Elise, who called to Nancy, who again turned Bright Beauty around to face the others, stopping the procession. "I can't see either, anymore, and I doubt the horses can. It'll be safer to wait out the heavy downpour."

Through twenty minutes of heavy sheets of driving rain, the riders sat on their mounts with heads bowed, water dripping from their helmet visors and shoulders. The saddles under them remained dry because the backs of their raincoats were draped over the cantle of the saddles to shed the water. Rain soaked through whatever blue jeans were exposed beyond the raincoats. The horses stood, heads bowed, eyes closed, rain soaking through their hair to their skin.

No one spoke until the rain slowed enough to see thirty feet in front of them. "Ready to go?" Nancy asked. "I want to get back to camp and get dry."

The others agreed and Nancy led them down the trail. They came to a steep hill that looked slippery. At the top, Nancy stopped and turned to the others. "Let's go down one at a time in case someone has a wreck. We'll wait at the bottom until everyone is down safely." She turned Bright Beauty back to face the hill and squeezed with her knees. Beauty went over. When she began sliding on all four legs, she sat on her rear end and walked with her front legs as her rump slid down the hill. Nancy sat with her weight toward the rear of her saddle to help the horse. They made it to the bottom without mishap. Nancy moved off a little way and turned to watch the others.

Tucker was only a quarter of the way down with Elise when Jolene was no longer able to hold Tricked Out back. Trick did not want to be left. He pranced and danced as he tried to follow his barn buddy over the top of the hill. Jolene turned his rump to the hill to prevent him from going over the edge, but the horse began going down backward. Jolene decided it was safer to allow him to go, instead of fighting him to wait. She turned him around and he continued his downhill slide frontwards.

Lavern and Lacy were last. Lacy slowly and carefully placed each of her hooves, and with a lot of sliding, they also made it to the bottom safely.

By the time they were back at camp, the rain had ceased. The women unsaddled, rubbed their horses down, cleaned out their hooves, gave them water, and put them on the picket line with fresh hay. Only then did they dry themselves off and put on dry clothes.

Usually the group ate lunch on the trail, but with the rain, they had taken the shortest way back to camp without stopping to eat. Jolene went to Nancy's trailer, then to Lavern's, and asked them to bring their lunches to eat together. "Come over to our trailer and eat with Mom and me."

They gathered around the picnic table under Elise's awning. The rain water dripped from their awnings and the trees, but it had quit falling from the sky, which had turned blue. The air smelled fresh and clean.

Nancy said a short grace after first asking if anyone else

wanted to. They chatted amicably while they ate.

"Has anyone heard from Bristol?" Nancy asked.

"No, the last I saw of her was when she left Harrison Forest that time she was so angry at us. I never heard from her after that." Lavern munched on a carrot stick.

"I never heard from her again, either," Elise agreed. "Hey, you know what?" Elise turned to Lavern. "I bet it was Bristol who informed your husband, what's his name, Charlie, where we were camping after she left. She sure was mad, and who else could have told Charlie?"

"I've thought about that a lot. Yes, either Bristol told him, or else he went to all the horsemen's camps we had ever been to in the past searching for me, and since we weren't there, he began widening the search to places we hadn't been to before. Not likely. I don't see him going all the way to Harrison Forest if he wasn't sure we were there."

Jolene broke in, "It is a distance, but he was on his motorcycle. Doesn't he love to ride it?"

"Well, there's that," Lavern agreed. "I still think he knew we were there."

"And Bristol was the only other person who knew where we were," Jolene finished for the group.

All heads nodded in agreement.

Sixteen months ago, Charlie became more abusive toward Lavern to the point that she became afraid of him. She left him, and he tried to take her horse trailer and horse. Slade, who owns Buckeye Farm where Lavern boards Lacy, stopped him with a shotgun and a call to the sheriff. Lavern found an apartment in a locked building, dropped off her previously boxed up belongings there, and called her friends to meet her at Harrison Forest without telling anyone where they would be.   Charlie came for her, demanded that she return home with him on the back of his bike, and became violent when she refused to leave with him. He hit Lavern, knocked Nancy down, and punched the forest ranger who had dropped by the camp and witnessed the whole incident. Because it was not Charlie's first domestic violence offense, he ended up in prison for assaulting the women and the law enforcement officer.

Lavern and her friends were hoping Charlie would receive a maximum prison sentence, but the prosecutor told Lavern that Charlie was willing to plead guilty to a reduced sentence of four years. The prosecutor had threatened him with the maximum of eleven years for the assault on Officer Jenkins, plus eight years for the domestic assault. He did not mention that if convicted, the sentences would probably run concurrently, or that Charlie probably would not receive the maximum. Charlie took the deal instead of taking the chance with a judge and jury.

Elise swallowed the last bite of her sandwich. "Well, I'm more comfortable without Bristol being around. She was always so snippy and sarcastic. I felt like I had to be careful of what I said. And when she turned on Jolene, that was way too much."

"Mom, you really stuck up for me. Then she almost ran over your foot! She sure was angry. I'm happier, too, that she doesn't come with us on our camping trips anymore."

"But, I hope that you have Bristol in your prayers, at least now and then. She has some kind of mental issues, I would think, and she must be a very unhappy person. She seems to have no self-confidence, and, I think, that's why she put others down so much." Nancy was the spiritual leader of the group.

Jolene frowned. "I don't get it. I mean, putting others down to raise yourself up? I don't understand that concept. It makes the person doing it look bad, not better."

"Exactly. So, pray for a healing for her."

"Oh, I think she has too much self-esteem and is over-confident. She acts like everyone else is beneath her." That was Lavern's take. "And she seems to want to get even with anyone she thinks disrespects her."

"Well, whatever, she needs your prayers for healing from her personality disorders." Nancy changed the subject. "Everyone finished? Let's pack up and go home."

...

Bristol detested doing the barn chores for her horse, Hot Stuff, a black and white Spotted Saddle Horse gelding. She loathed the odor of urine that was mixed in with the straw as she shoveled the heavy, dirty bedding into the wheelbarrow. The manure did not reek. It was almost a pleasant smell, but the manure, hay, and leather smells in the barn did not overcome the strong urine stench wafting up from the disturbed bedding as she shoveled. When she was married, Richard, or Ric, had done all the barn chores. Before she married Ric, she had boarded her horse.

Ric had left Bristol sixteen months ago. He filed for a divorce which was now final. They had agreed to sell their house with acreage and a horse barn, and to split the proceeds. It finally sold. She now had thirty days to leave the property to the new owners. She had already found a condominium her share of the sale of the property would pay for. She needed to find a boarding barn for Hot Stuff.

The wheelbarrow loads were heavy, difficult to push and dump. Bristol finished the last load and went into the house to make some calls. The sooner she could move Hot Stuff where someone else would do the work, the better. She began with the boarding barn where she had kept her first horses, Little Lady, then Blaze.

"Hi, I wondered if you have any stalls available? I need to find a place for my horse." Bristol paced her living room as she talked on her cell phone.

"Yes, we do. How did you hear about our barn?"

"Umm, I used to board there a while back. I'm Bristol Monarch. I ..."

Bristol was interrupted before she could finish.

"Oh, yes, I remember you. I'm sorry, I thought we had one stall available, but I see now, it's already promised." Click. The line went dead.

"Well! What's the matter with her?" Bristol grumbled to herself. She made two more calls and found an opening.

"Thank you, I'll bring the horse over today."

...

Lavern pulled the horse trailer into Buckeye Farm. She stopped in front of the barn to unload. As Lacy was stepping out with a clang of steel shoes on the ramp, Lavern looked around for Slade, but she did not see him.

She walked Lacy into the barn on the way to give her freedom in the pasture and a much-needed roll in the dirt. Slade was facing her, talking with a woman in the aisleway. "Hi, Slade." As she spoke, the woman turned around and Lavern stopped short.

"You! What are you doing here, Bristol?" Lavern was surprised to see her.

"Slade's been showing me the barn set up. I brought Hot Stuff here." Bristol turned back around to Slade and ignored Lavern.

"Have a good trip?" Slade asked Lavern.

"Yeah, Slade, it was good, even with the heavy rain earlier." She walked Lacy down the long aisle with stalls on both sides, and out to the pasture. *Oh, brother! I sure don't need this! Man! I hope she won't be around here much. What a way to ruin a day.*

Lavern opened the pasture gate and led Lacy through before removing her halter. "Freedom, Lacy. Have fun."

Lacy trotted off a short distance, sniffed the ground, went down, rolled to one side, then to the other side. She scooched around on her back, rolled again, stood up with a satisfied snort and a good shake that scattered dust into the air, then trotted toward the other horses. Lavern watched her for a few minutes before returning to unload the living quarters of her horse trailer. She had laundry and left-over food to take back to her apartment.

Bristol walked past as Lavern was unhitching. She glanced at Lavern without speaking. Lavern decided to take the high road and spoke, "How have you been, Bristol?"

"Oh, I've been fine. Life is good." Bristol kept walking.

Lavern, who did want to know, asked her, "How is Ric?" Everyone thought highly of Ric and wondered how he put up with

Bristol.

Bristol stopped then and turned toward Lavern without approaching her. "Like I said, life is good. No more Ric, no more bother."

"Are you divorced?" Lavern was only somewhat surprised to hear they were at least separated.

"Yes, so what?"

"So nothing, Bristol. Truly, nothing. I liked Ric, that's all, and wondered how he is."

"Well, you can have him. I'm done with him, and I heard you finally divorced Charlie."

I'd bet money that it's more like Ric was done with her. I wonder if she kept his name or reverted to her maiden name? I'll ask Slade what name she's using.

Bristol turned back in the direction she was heading without saying good-bye. Lavern said nothing more, either.

...

Elise and Jolene pulled into their driveway and drove the rig to the back where they could unload Tucker and Tricked Out next to the barn. Elise was glad to reach home before it was dark. They took care of the horses and went to the house.

Elise loved the house. It was custom built for her and her husband Marty by her father-in-law's company. She especially loved the wrap-around porch and the three-season sun room. She and Jolene took off their barn boots in the mud room and slipped into comfortable shoes.

"I'm going up to my room, Mom, to do some more research on colleges. Thanks for the weekend." Jolene hugged her mother and ran upstairs.

What am I going to do without her when she goes off to college? Mother and daughter had always had a close relationship that did not include Marty, by his choice. It was a marriage of necessity when Elise became pregnant at sixteen. The Parkers provided well for her and Jolene. Marty finished high school, attended a local college, graduated, and began working for the family contracting and construction business. They had a good income and Marty did not question any of her expenditures. She had everything that she wanted except for love. She and Marty lived in the same house but lived separate lives.

Elise felt a loneliness not being able to love, trust, and share with a devoted partner. She craved mutual passion, tenderness, respect, and caring with someone who loved and cherished her the way Harry loved Nancy.

She walked through the silent house and wondered where Marty was now, although she did not really care. She went upstairs to take a hot, soaking, bubble bath and relax. Before she could draw the water, her phone rang.

"Hi, it's Lavern. You'll never guess what!"

"Well, then, you better tell me." Elise sat on her bed in her robe to talk.

"Bristol was at Buckeye Farm when I got there. She's boarding her horse there now."

"That's not good news for you. Did you talk with her?" Elise studied her nails and decided they needed attention.

"Yeah, we barely spoke, but she did tell me she and Ric are divorced. Man, I sure hope she won't be around there much."

"I know what you mean. Hey, did you find out if she kept Ric's name?"

"Yeah, I asked Slade. She's still using Monarch. I guess she likes being royalty too much to give it up."

Elise chuckled. "I was thinking, good, her initials are still B.M."

They talked briefly, and Elise hung up to soak in her bubbles.

...

Before the women left camp for home, Nancy prayed for them to be safe on their journeys. She used the drive home to pray for her friends and family. She asked for healing for Bristol from whatever made her so venal. She asked for comfort and acceptance for Lavern for the loss of her parents and brother in a horrible traffic accident. She prayed that Lavern would again come to feel close to the Lord. She asked God to help Elise find fulfillment in her life. She prayed for other friends in her life and for her family. She asked for her own acceptance of her father's death from a sudden heart attack and her mother's Alzheimer's disease. She asked God to bless her mother with the ability to stay home for a long time and enjoy her remaining life, and to bless her sister for having come home to help her care for their mother. She thanked God for her adoring, thoughtful, helpful husband. Then she started on the country, its president, and the world, asking for peace and healings.

By the time she pulled in her driveway, she had no one left to pray for.

Harry came out of the house to meet her and help her unload. He gave her a big, warm hug when she jumped down from the truck.

"Have fun?" He put his hands on her shoulders. "Let me look at you. I missed you."

"Yeah, we had fun. We always do. How was Mom? Did she give you and Sis any trouble?" Her sister, Abigail, lived with them in the Stouffer family home where she and Nancy grew up. Don and Mary Stouffer, their parents, had sold the property to Harry Reynolds and Nancy when they married. Don and Mary moved to a house in the small town of Ravenna in Portage County. Don died, and Nancy and Harry moved Mary back to the Stouffer home when her Alzheimer's disease progressed to the point she could no longer live alone.

"No more than usual. It's OK. As always, we watched her closely to keep her safe. It's good to be retired and have the time. Let's get Bright Beauty unloaded."

Harry helped with the horse and with unloading the living quarters. Nancy was grateful for his help.

When she came into the house, Mary asked, "Who's this? Who are you? Don't sit down. I want to watch TV."

Nancy sat next to her mother and took her hand. "Look at me, Mom. I'm your daughter, Nancy. We live here together. We can watch the TV together. It's all right."

Abigail came into the living room. "How was the trip?"

"Hi, Sis. It was fun, as always. Still, I'm glad to be home, but I'll be ready to go horse camping with the girls again next month. I have to get in enough day rides to keep Bright Beauty in shape. I sure am glad I'm retired."

"You're going camping in November? In the cold?"
Abigail shivered at the thought.

"Probably. It depends on the weather. It shouldn't be that
cold. The living quarters in all our trailers have a furnace, and
we'll dress warm. The horses love to move out in the cooler
weather. It's fun."

"It reminds me of the time Dad took you and me to the
horse auction in Pennsylvania for that weekend in April when our
trailer furnace wasn't working. It was kind of fun. Oh, I almost
forgot to tell you. While you were out back at the barn, Lavern
called. She said to tell you Bristol is boarding Hot Stuff at
Buckeye Farm now, and that she and Ric are divorced."

"Well, that's some news, Sis. Umm."

Mary said, "Shh," and Nancy squeezed her mother's hand,
kissed her forehead, and left the room to return Lavern's call.

...

Chapter Two

Brewing Trouble

Bristol watched and listened as she groomed Hot Stuff in the crossties in the barn aisle. She wanted to know who was popular among the boarders, and how much Lavern was liked or disliked. She could tip the scale toward dislike if she figured out the right people to talk to.

Alexa, one of the boarders, needed to pass to have access to her stall farther down the aisle. "Does he kick?"

"No, you can go by."

Alexa put her left hand on Hot Stuff's rump to let him know she was there, so he would not be startled and possibly kick. She ducked under the crossties that were anchored on the two sides of the aisle. "He's pretty. What is he?"

Bristol smiled. It still gave her pleasure when someone acknowledged the beauty of her horse. "He's a Spotted Saddle Horse. Yes, he is pretty, but you should have seen him after Lavern cut off his tail. It took a long time to grow back, too. Do you know Lavern Smith?"

"Why would she do that? That doesn't sound like Lavern. Oh, she's Lavern Esser now."

"I don't want to talk about it. It brings back bad memories." Bristol turned her back on Alexa and smirked. *First point. Score!*

Hot Stuff's tail had not been cut off, or cut at all. Lavern was never involved in the practical joke Jolene, her boyfriend Randy, and two other women, Bree and Cadey, played on Bristol at Harrison Forest. There was a large knot at the top of Bree's horse's tail. Bree and Cadey had to cut it out. Streaming down from the tangled mess were long, straight hairs not caught in the knot. It was black hair, the color of Hot Stuff's tail. Randy placed the large hank of hair under Hot Stuff as the horse stood on the picket line. The four players managed to talk about stress and hair loss during the pot luck supper. When Bristol returned to her horse, she immediately thought it was Hot Stuff's tail. When she saw the others laughing while watching her, she knew she had been pranked. It had not been done maliciously, but Bristol did not see the humor in it.

...

Lavern used a key to open the door to her building, picked up her mail from her box in the row of mail boxes in the lobby, and used another key to unlock her apartment door on the third floor. She had been lucky to find it in a hurry the day she left Charlie. She liked the idea of living behind two locked doors to be safe from Charlie. It was furnished with furniture borrowed from Nancy's sister, Abigail, when she had moved in with Nancy and Harry. The loan would keep Abigail from having to pay storage fees until she needed it back. By then, Lavern would have enough savings to buy her own.

Inside the door was a hallway, more of a vestibule. A coat closet was behind sliding doors the length of the short hallway that opened into her living room. The open concept kitchen was to the right, separated from the living room by a narrow island with two bar stools. The bedroom and small bathroom were off the other end. The living room had sliding glass doors leading onto a balcony barely large enough for two folding lawn chairs. Lavern hung up her jacket, walked into her living room, and was about to toss her mail onto the end table next to her favorite chair, when she noticed a letter from the prison parole board.

Holy smokes! What's this?

The rest of the mail and her purse dropped to the floor as she tore open the critical envelope and read the letter. She sat down and reread the letter, but it said the same thing. Charlie was getting out of prison on an early release due to overcrowding.

That quickly, Lavern's world was turned upside down. She no longer felt safe at home, school, or anywhere, and she feared for the safety of her horse.

Well, Charlie doesn't know where I live, and I could always move Lacy. Bristol's at Buckeye Farm now, anyway, but I don't want to leave Slade. I love that old man!

Lavern jumped up, retrieved her purse and the rest of the mail. She tossed the mail onto the table and dug her cell phone out of her purse to call Nancy. Abigail answered. Nancy was out back in the barn. Lavern left a message with her, hung up, and called Elise.

She paced as she talked. "Elise, there's a big problem. Charlie is being released early because of overcrowding. I'm afraid he hasn't been in long enough to forget about me and go on with his life. I don't know what to do."

"He doesn't know where you live now, and the building is secure. I wouldn't worry too much about him. Just be aware of your surroundings all the time the way we're supposed to be anyway. I'll pray for your safety."

"I appreciate that, Elise. I don't think he'd come around you and Jolene, but you two should be more cautious than normal. He knows you're my friends, and who knows how he might want to get even with me."

Her next call was to Slade who told her not to worry about Lacy. "I'll do that for you, Missy. If he comes around your sweet mare, he'll end up with buckshot in his arse. You take care of yourself. Stay on alert when you're out and about."

When Nancy returned Lavern's call, Lavern shared her fears.

"That's why you live where you do, behind two locked doors. Be on high alert when out and about. I'll pray for no harm to come to you."

"Thanks, Nancy. I'll be praying, too. I loved Charlie before he became abusive. I loved who he was when he was charming and not controlling. I would like to be happy for him to be free again, but I'm worried about him finding me, plus, what about Lacy? Will he try to get even with me by hurting her? He tried to take her once before."

"I don't know. We'll pray for Lacy's safety, too. Slade will watch out for her. Be sure to tell Slade about Charlie's release."

"Oh, I did, right away. I should probably notify my school, too. I'd hate for him to come after me there. Geez, all those school shootings! I hate to think the kids might not be safe because of me. You be careful, too, my friend, in case. Well, I'll let you go. I know you're busy with your mother. I just wanted you to know about Charlie. Thanks for the prayers."

The next day, Lavern notified her school principal. She

hoped she would not be fired because of Charlie. She loved her teaching job.

...

Elise brought the mail in. She sorted it on the kitchen counter. She had an invitation for a free hearing exam that she dumped in the trash. Marty had utility bills, and Jolene had a letter.

Jolene was propped on the wicker chaise lounge in the sunroom, barefoot, reading her history homework. Elise took her the letter.

"Look what I have! Want to know who it's from?" Elise waved the letter, teasing.

"It has to be from Randy. Who else writes me letters? Everybody else emails or texts. Let me have it." Jolene reached for it, but Elise put it behind her back.

"Who's going to do the dishes tonight?" she teased.

"Ah, Mom, give it to me. I always load the dishwasher and run it."

Elise gave her Randy's letter and sat on the wicker chair across from her daughter. She loved this room with the wicker furniture, a pattern of bright yellow sunflowers and yellow and orange butterflies on the cushions, and the glass top on the round wicker table where she kept a vase full of yellow, orange, red, and pink zinnias mid-summer through the first frost. The ceiling fan helped cool it in the summer, and the electric fireplace kept it warm in the spring and fall. Today the golden sunshine gave it enough warmth.

"Well, come on. Open it up. Let's hear what he has to say."

"Mom!" Jolene turned the word into two syllables. "I'm not reading it aloud until I've read it to myself." Now it was Jolene's turn to tease. "Then I'll keep all the juicy parts to myself."

Elise and Jolene met Randy while riding at Quail Hollow State Park the summer before last. Jolene and Randy dated the rest of that summer until Randy went back to college. He was studying to become a veterinarian. They wrote during that school year and dated again all this past summer.

"OK, then, I'll go bake some cookies and give you time to read your letter. Your dad likes my chocolate chip cookies with double the chocolate and double the walnuts."

Elise was half way up when Jolene stopped her. "Mom, I've been wanting to ask you something for a long time."

Elise, always ready to give her daughter her full attention, sat back down. "What, Honey? You know you can ask me anything."

"Yeah, I know, but this is personal, and I haven't asked because I thought it might be too private for you to talk about." Jolene closed the unopened letter inside her history book.

"Boy, this sounds serious. How about we make a deal? You ask, but I don't have to answer."

"Good deal, Mom. That makes me feel better about asking." Jolene hugged the book against her chest as though to create a barrier between them, maybe a little more privacy where there was about to be less.

"OK, here goes." She took a deep breath, but said nothing.

"If you've thought about it for a long time, how come you can't spit it out? Just say it, Honey."

"OK, OK, umm. Well, like, OK. I got it. Nancy and Harry, you can see they really love each other, right?

Elise nodded agreement.

"You can see they love and respect each other. Then there was Charlie. He seemed to love Lavern too much. Like, so much that he had to control her, like he was jealous or didn't trust her, or something. I mean, if he didn't love her, he wouldn't care what she did or where she went."

"Yes, go on." Elise was a bit afraid of where this conversation was headed.

"OK, so, where on the spectrum are you and Dad? You don't do things together except to go to the Parker family events sometimes. I mean, you don't act like you love each other, and he doesn't act like he cares about what we do or where we go. Is that because he trusts you and respects you, or is it because, because …"

"You can say it. Is it because he doesn't love me, doesn't care?"

Jolene was relieved to have her mother say it for her. "Yeah, I was wondering. I never saw any affection between you, but he's never mean the way Charlie was. But he seems indifferent. Does he love you? Does he love us? Did he ever love you?" I know you always told me you and dad dated after you were out of school, but I know how old you were when you had me. I can do the math. I'm seventeen, and you're barely thirty-four. You had me when you were seventeen."

"Oh, boy. I was afraid you would figure this out." Elise hesitated while trying to think how to phrase what she wanted to say. Jolene waited.

Elise admitted, "I turned seventeen just before you were born. Your father finished high school and went to college. I graduated with a GED diploma. We married shortly after you were born. This is why I've always cautioned you to wait for sex until you're married. I want you to have a choice who and when to marry, then have babies after you're married. Sex should be an expression of love for each other."

"So, do you and Dad love each other? You've always been a great homemaker. I mean, look at this house and the way you keep it. You make good meals and bake special things like the cookies, but Dad doesn't thank you for anything. Most of the time he isn't even here. I don't think I've ever had a real discussion with him. He says OK to anything I ask for, but he doesn't talk with me or do anything with me, or you either."

She really wants to know if her own father loves her. What can I say?

"He was dating another girl, but he broke it off with her and married me." *Would this be enough to satisfy her?*

"But do you love each other?"

"He may be a little resentful that he had to marry so young, but look how he treats us, Honey. He does allow us to do what we want, when we want, no questions asked. He provides very well for us. Your college will be paid for, we have our beautiful home, and our horses, truck and trailer. We've had a new car every three years for the two of us, and you'll get a new car of your own when you go off to college. So, yes, I'll bake him chocolate chip cookies and prepare nice meals. Sometimes, no most times, actions speak louder than words. Would you rather have a man who doesn't treat you well, but who says he loves you? Or one who never says he loves you, but treats you very well?"

"Why can't you have both in a man? That's what I want."

"That's what I want for you, too, Sweetheart. Like Harry and Nancy." Elise continued, "You know, I'm not sure Dad knows how to be the father you're looking for. Maybe you're going to have to take the initiative to hold conversations with him."

Providing well for us is different than showing us love, Jolene thought.

Harry and Nancy. It's what I want for myself, too, but I'll never have it, Elise thought.

...

Mary was returning from the bathroom to her bedroom. She wore only her bra and underpants. Her robe was left lumped on the bathroom floor.

Harry turned the corner from the living room to the hallway to go to the bathroom and stopped short. He had no desire to see his mother-in-law this way. Before he could turn himself around, Mary peeked over her shoulder at him, winked, and walked into her bedroom.

"Nancy! Abigail! We could use a little help here," he called, hoping one of the sisters was within hearing distance.

Abigail was in the basement, and Nancy was out back in the barn.

Harry went on into the bathroom, then back to the living

room. Mary sat in front of the TV, still only in her bra and panties. Harry turned around to go out the back door to find Nancy when Abigail came up the basement steps with jars of tomato juice canned from Harry's garden.

"Umm, you better, ah, better go tend to your mother. She's in the living room." Harry rushed outside.

He found Nancy in the barn brushing Bright Beauty who stood quietly in the cross ties enjoying it.

"Hi, Honey, how come you're out here with no jacket. It's a little cool." Nancy kept brushing her horse.

"Well, ah, it got a bit, ah, unnerving in the house."

"What? Everything OK? What happened?"

"Your mother was going around the house wearing only her underwear. Don't worry. Abigail is handling it. I know Mary, the Mary we all used to know before this disease took over, would be so embarrassed to have me see her that way. I left her to Abigail."

Harry searched around, found another brush, and began brushing Bright Beauty's other side. Nancy and Harry enjoyed the peace of the barn together in silence.

...

Chapter Three

First Week in November

Bristol's daughter, Sophia, detested calling her mother, especially to ask for help of any kind. Bristol had never wanted a child and had never grown to love or appreciate her daughter, nor did she care to be active in her grandchild's life.

When Bristol's cell phone rang disturbing her enjoyment of reading a novel, she checked the number and almost did not answer when Sophia's name appeared.

"What?" was her greeting.

"Mother, I hate to bother you, and I wouldn't if I weren't in dire straits."

Before Sophia could explain, Bristol interrupted. "Don't come to me for money. You know I'm retired."

"No, I'm not. It's Jenny. She has a bad cold, so I can't take her to day care. Dad's out of town, my normal babysitter has the flu, and I have to go to work. I was hoping that you would watch her tomorrow. It's Friday, so it would only be the one day. She should be better by Monday, and anyway, Dad will be back Sunday night. I only need help for tomorrow, so I can go to work."

Bristol said nothing.

After a short pause, Sophia asked, "So, Mother, can I drop her off with you tomorrow morning?"

Bristol put her bookmark in place and closed the novel. "Absolutely not. I don't babysit. I told you that the day you told me you were pregnant. What would I do with the kid all day?"

"With this cold, she'll probably sleep most of the day. You can read to her, make her lunch, play with a puzzle. I can send some books and toys with her. You seldom see her, Mother, but that's by your choice. You're missing out on something precious. You could bond with your grandchild over the horses. She would love to go to the barn and see all the horses when she doesn't have a cold."

"I'm not babysitting. I sleep in now that I'm retired. I don't want to get up early. You'll have to find someone else." Bristol changed the subject. "Why is your father out of town? Where did he go?"

"I'm sorry, Mother, but I'm not going to talk about either one of you to the other. If you want to know, you'll have to ask him."

"Well, aren't you the bratty kid? And here you are trying to have me do you a favor. I think not." Bristol hung up and opened her novel. She wanted to read one more chapter then practice her new song with her guitar.

She was having trouble concentrating on her reading. She kept wondering whether Ric had a girlfriend. Did he take her on a weekend trip? Where was he living now?

...

Charlie Smith had sold his Honda motorcycle to a buddy, Brian Myers, to pay for his legal fees. Now on parole with an early release from prison, Charlie was bunking in Brian's second bedroom and borrowing the motorcycle until he could find employment. His parole officer told Charlie that finding housing would be difficult. The landlords frowned on renting to those with prison records. Employment with a record could also be difficult, but Charlie had immediately called his boss from his old company and was given an interview appointment. They had always liked him there because he knew how to pour on the charm, and he had always been their top salesman. Hopefully they would take him back.

As Charlie rode the red Honda toward the school where Lavern had been teaching when he went to prison, he hoped that she was still teaching there. He also hoped that he would be given back his old job. Riding the bike was chilly this time of year. He needed to buy a car and to begin paying rent to Brian.

He parked the bike across from the school. *I only want to make sure this is still where she teaches. Make no trouble, no trouble, no trouble.*

As he crossed the street, he wondered if the school doors would be locked. They were not. Inside, he looked right, then left. Seeing a sign for the office with an arrow pointing to the left, he walked down the hall.

The office door was standing open. He entered and stood in front of a long counter. Behind it, two women were seated at desks. They each looked up from their work.

One spoke. "Can I help you?" She stood and approached the counter.

"Umm, yes, thank you. I need to speak with your teacher, Mrs. Smith." Charlie jingled the coins in his jeans pocket.

"We don't have a Mrs. Smith teaching here. We do have

…," the woman was interrupted by the other one.

"Zelda! No, Zelda. Umm, we have no Mrs. Smith here. Sorry." She, too, approached the counter. "What is your name?"

Instead of answering, Charlie said, "I guess I have the wrong school. Sorry. Have a nice day, ladies." He turned and left.

Adrianna turned to her co-worker. "You were about to tell him we have a Miss Esser who used to be Mrs. Smith, weren't you? Couldn't you guess that was Charlie Smith, Lavern's ex-husband? You need to be much more careful!"

Both women hurried to the windows flanking the length of one end of the office. "Look, there he goes." Zelda pointed and Adrianna nodded as they watched Charlie buckle on a helmet and climb on the Honda.

The principal came out of her adjoining office and observed the two secretaries at the windows. "What's going on?"

"We think Charlie Smith was here trying to find Lavern," Adrianna answered. "He just drove off on a motorcycle."

"This is not good. Tell me what happened. What did you tell him? What did he say?"

After explaining, the principal asked them to have Lavern come to the office at her earliest convenience.

Lavern confirmed that it must have been Charlie. Charlie did have a red motorcycle, and there was no one else who would be searching for her.

The principal decided they would begin keeping the school doors locked from the outside. She asked Zelda to send a letter to the parents explaining they would have to telephone the school to make an appointment if they needed to come in, and to apologize for any inconvenience.

As soon as Lavern finished her teaching day, she headed for Buckeye Farm. She found Slade throwing hay bales from the upstairs loft to the aisle below. She called up to him.

"Slade, I need to talk to you. I'm coming up."

Before Lavern could climb the ladder, Slade told her he would come down. They sat on two of the hay bales in the aisle.

"I'm so worried, Slade. I'm actually kind of scared. Charlie came to my school today, trying to find me. I don't know what he wants, but it scares me. He tried to take Lacy, and I sure don't want him to try again. He might be successful. I couldn't bear to think he might take her to a slaughter house." She put her head in her hands, her elbows on her knees. She was still dressed in the skirt and blouse she had worn in her classroom instead of in the usual blue jeans she wore to the barn.

Slade shook his head and frowned. "I don't like that he's looking for you. I hoped he would leave you alone. Well, Missy, you take care of yourself. Get you some fresh pepper spray and always watch your surroundings. I'll take care of your mare."

"You won't always be around, Slade. I mean, you could be in town or working somewhere else on the farm when he shows up." Lavern looked up through her long lashes where two tear drops were caught.

"I'll tell you what we'll do." Slade spit tobacco juice. "We'll change Lacy's stall to the empty one third from the end. She's usually out in the pasture anyway, but I'll take her name plate off the door and not put it on the other stall. If he comes around, it will look like she isn't here anymore."

"Yeah, I like that idea." Lavern moved her hands and held her head up. "Maybe I can park my horse trailer at one of my friend's house. He'd be much more inclined to believe she's not here if my trailer's gone, too."

"Right. Then we'll put her in the back pasture with the retired horses, so he won't even see her. She'll be fine. Don't worry none about her, Missy. Get that trailer moved and watch yourself. Keep that pepper spray handy. I'll still loan you my gun, if you'll take it."

"No, no guns, but thank you, Slade. And thanks for all your help."

...

Elise and Jolene sat side by side in front of the desk in Jolene's bedroom. They were searching colleges on line.

"It would help if you knew a course of study. What do you want for a career? You could choose your college by the programs they offer. I wanted to be a lawyer …"

"Really, Mom? You wanted to be a lawyer?" Jolene was amazed. "I didn't know that. Why didn't you go for it?"

"That's a long story. So, anyway, I wanted to be a lawyer, and I was going to go to Kent State. I found out they have pre-law, but no law school. My point is, you need to know a major or a career to help you pick a college."

Jolene leaned back in her chair and put her hands behind her head. She sighed. "I don't know. I don't want to go into medicine. I'm not especially good in science or math, even though my grades are good. It's a struggle to keep them up in those areas. I enjoy English and history, but what would you do with English? Teach? What about history? Teach or politics? Not for me."

"What were the results of the aptitude test you took in school?"

"It said I should work with animals or work in the outdoors. It suggested construction, landscaping, park ranger, marine biologist, pet grooming, veterinarian or vet tech, animal control officer, and a few other choices I can't remember. I might like to be a vet, but I'm not good with balancing chemistry equations. I wouldn't be good with seeing sick animals all the time, either. How depressing! I'd be OK with horses for things like vaccinations to keep them well, but I wouldn't want to see them suffering and sick. What am I going to do with my life, Mom?"

"Don't worry about it, Honey. It will come to you. You can always start college with general studies until you figure out your major. What did you think about your grandfather's proposal?"

Jolene's Grandfather Parker had offered her a position in the family business if she would major in something related.

"I don't know. Maybe. I'd have to take business and computer classes. Those could serve me well in other areas, too. I might work for him this summer between high school and college. I'd get a feel for working there to help me make up my mind. The only thing is, it would cut down on my riding time." Jolene frowned.

Elise had an idea. "What's your favorite thing to do?"

"Ride my horse. Camp with the horses. Hang out doing

33

stuff with the horses. Why?"

"Let's explore jobs that involve horses." When Jolene frowned, Elise continued, "Why not? It won't hurt to look."

They focused back on the computer and began a search. Elise was enjoying working with Jolene on her college search, but it did make her wistful for her own lost college experience and a law career.

...

Abigail Stouffer had never been married. Over the years, she dated several doctors from the hospital where she worked. None of them ever seemed to be the man of her dreams. She often wondered whether she read too many romance novels that glorified the sexy hero as too perfect. That was who she was looking for, and she believed he could exist because Nancy found a man like that in her husband, Harry Reynolds.

Tonight, she was dressing in her favorite black slacks with a cream silk blouse and shiny black bolero jacket paired with short-heeled black sandals. The outfit made her appear taller and thinner. She had a date with a man who, so far, could be the one. She was seventy-two and had given up on marriage. She was willing to settle for the company of an intelligent, thought-provoking man, who would take her to dinner and a movie. She met Lawrence Wright at a book club meeting at the Ravenna Library the month before. Larry, as he preferred to be called, was a widower of four years, who was also looking for intelligent, stimulating companionship.

They exchanged telephone numbers and talked several times before tonight's book club meeting. Larry offered to pick her up for the meeting. She agreed.

As Abigail was applying her lipstick, Nancy knocked and entered her bedroom. "Hey, Sis, are you excited? You know he has to come in and meet us, or you can't go out with him."

"Oh, he will. He's a gentleman. Yeah, I guess I'm kind of excited. You wouldn't think I would be at my age, but still ..." Abigail picked up small gold hoop earrings and put them into her ears. "I only have two other nice outfits. I wore scrubs at work, and here I only wear jeans. If this works out, come shopping with me and help me find some pretty clothes."

"Of course, that'll be fun."

The doorbell rang, and the sisters went into the living room. Harry opened the door, and a tall, handsome man with salt and pepper hair stepped in. Harry offered his hand and introduced himself.

"It's good to meet you, Harry. I'm Larry Wright."

"Please come in. Here's Sis, uh, Abigail."

Abigail took Larry's elbow and with her other hand, pointed to her sister. "This is my sister, Nancy, and my mother, Mary, is seated on the sofa."

Nancy and Larry shook hands and exchanged greetings. Mary stared at the television.

"Come on in and sit down for a few minutes." Abigail pointed to a chair. "Would you like some coffee?"

"No thank you, I'm fine." Larry took the seat and Abigail sat near him. Harry and Nancy sat on the sofa with Mary.

"No! Get up! You can't have it!" Mary protectively held

her purple, toy puppy away from Nancy.

"No, Mom, I don't want it. It's yours. Settle down. I want to talk with Sis's new friend."

Mary jumped up and hurried down the hall to her bedroom.

After a few awkward attempts, the conversation began to flow. Harry related how he met Nancy in the local Walmart store, how her family spied on that meeting, and how he had fallen and knocked over the donut display. Larry genuinely laughed.

Nancy asked Larry what some of his interests were. He enjoyed thoughtful books, inspiring movies, and good meals in nicer restaurants.

Nancy told how she and Abigail liked horses and how they came by their first horse when their father went out to buy a piano and came home with a horse instead. Again, Larry laughed sincerely.

They were enjoying each other's company, but it was time to leave for their meeting. Larry and Abigail said their good-byes and left.

"That went well," Nancy said to Harry. "I liked him. Did you?"

"Time will tell, but yes, as of tonight, he seems nice."

"I hope this is the beginning of something special for Sis. She deserves it."

...

Chapter Four

Second Week in November

It was a rare, crisp, November day with the high temperature predicted to reach seventy-two. At nine-thirty in the morning, the sun was already bright in a clear sky of turquoise blue. Bristol wanted to take advantage of the beautiful weather before it turned nasty for the winter season, but she was tired of riding alone.

She had not talked with Ric's sister, Geri Monarch, since Ric had left sixteen months earlier. Bristol had felt that it was up to Geri to reach out to commiserate with her when Ric left. After all, Geri had been her friend since before she married Ric. Geri did not contact her, and Bristol, holding it against her, refused to call Geri.

Now she wondered whether she was justified in her anger toward Geri. It was Ric who left her, not Geri. *No, Geri left me, too, when she never called me again. Anyway, I want someone to ride with.*

Bristol was conflicted whether or not to call Geri now to see if she would be willing to meet her at the trailhead in Cuyahoga Valley National Park to ride. Her curiosity about Ric won out, and she made the call. Geri might be willing to tell her what Ric was up to now.

"Hi, Geri. It's Bristol. It's a great day to ride. Want to go?" Bristol took her coffee to the kitchen island and sat on a bar stool.

"Bristol? Gee, I'm surprised to hear from you." Bristol could not tell from Geri's tone whether she was pleased or not.

"Well, yeah, I guess so, but how about a ride today? We could catch up with each other. This is going to be one of the last nice days of the year, maybe the best day left." She sipped her coffee.

"It's kind of last minute, Bristol."

"True, but you were always spontaneous. Let's meet at the Wetmore Trail Head in the Cuyahoga Valley, say, in two hours?"

"Come on, Bristol, in all this time you never called me until today when you want some company. Are you feeling lonely? Have you alienated everyone in your life now? Don't you have any friends anymore? I wish I had never introduced you to my brother, or to my friends in the horse club. You are a toxic person, Bristol. You make people so miserable. My brother was so good to you, and you never appreciated all he did for you. You only said mean things to him and about him."

"Really! Who's toxic? You're talking about yourself. Listen to the nasty things you just said about me. Who do you think you are? You were supposed to be my friend, and you never called me to see how I was doing after Ric left me, like you didn't care." Bristol slammed the phone shut and threw the rest of her coffee into the sink. It had turned acidic in her stomach.

I'll go out to the farm and see who's there to ride with or go by myself. I'm not wasting this day. I don't need Geri or anyone else.

Only two other boarders were at Buckeye Farm when Bristol arrived. Neither of them was inclined to ride with Bristol. She rode alone, again.

...

Charlie sat in front of the school in the used car he bought after getting his old job back in computer sales. It had been easy. He knew how to be charming, he had always been well-liked at work, and being the top money earner was the deciding factor. His boss was glad to have him back.

The two old biddies, who must have been the school secretaries, tried to cover the fact that Lavern taught there, but he could see they were flustered. The one seemed about to tell him something when the other quickly interrupted her. He thought she might have been about to say they did have a Miss Esser who used to be Mrs. Smith. *Yeah, I think she still teaches here.*

He watched as parents continued to drive up and park along the side of the road to pick up their children. The yellow school buses were lined up in the circular drive in front of the school. He checked his watch. Children should be leaving soon, and the teachers would soon follow. He picked up the binoculars to double check the focus looking into the teachers' parking lot. He was not sure which door Lavern would exit, but he would see her going to her vehicle. She must have bought a car while he was in prison because he did not see her truck.

Fifteen minutes after the buses and cars left with the children, the teachers began to trickle out. Charlie kept the binoculars to his eyes searching for Lavern. He needed to see what vehicle she was driving now. He planned to follow her to find out where she was living. Later, he would decide what to do next.

Is that her? Yeah, I think it is! "You pretty little bitch. Come to Daddy."

Charlie watched through his binoculars as Lavern and another woman walked to a green Hyundai Sonata. Lavern went to the passenger side, and the other woman got behind the wheel.

"Huh, did your truck break down, or do you ride share with her?" he mumbled. He did not like the idea of another person around. It would make approaching Lavern more difficult. He wanted no witnesses. Dropping the binoculars onto the seat, he started the engine.

The Sonata pulled out of the school driveway and headed right. Charlie was on the street headed in the opposite direction. By the time he turned his car around, the Sonata was out of sight. He traveled the road trying to catch up, but he did not see it again. *Maybe they turned off. There's always another day. I have nothing but time. Maybe I'll drive out to Buckeye Farm and see what's what out there.*

...

Jolene and Elise looked at Ohio State programs. The school offered Animal Sciences, Livestock Production and Management, Horse Production and Management, and Randy.

"I would love to go to the same school as Randy, Mom, but he's so busy with his veterinary studies, I wouldn't see much of him, anyway. I don't see much for me here except for Randy. Let's try some others."

They were on Jolene's computer again. When Jolene took a bathroom break and went downstairs for a cup of tea, Elise began searching law schools. Kent State had pre-law, but still no law school. The University of Akron had a law school. *What am I doing? This is only pipe dreaming. Well, I can play for a few minutes.*

Jolene returned with her cup of tea. Elise closed the web site she was on.

They discovered Hocking Hills Technical College. It offered an Associate of Applied Science in Wilderness Horsemanship that could be earned in four semesters.

"Mom, look how much of the curriculum I already know from our years of trail riding! It lists procedures with tack, OK, check, proper horse care, check, basic horse health, check, managing unmounted horse including leading, tying, duh, trailer loading, transporting, catching, check, manage horse without assistance mounting, dismounting, duh, trail skills, and handling horses at walk, trot, canter, all terrain, duh! I know this stuff! It's what we do! I'd be spending time and Dad's money to earn the paper that says I can do it."

"Yes, that, while having fun, and see, there's leather craft as related to tack, plus proper care and handling of pack stock and packing equipment. That would all be new for you, then the equine business part must have basic business classes valuable in any business."

Jolene sipped her tea, thinking. "Look, there's also shoeing on this list. I don't want to be a blacksmith. It's too hard on your back, but if your horse loses a shoe on trail, it would be good to be able to, like, handle it yourself." Excited, Jolene asked, "Can we click on the button to set up a visit to the college? I mean, I'm not sure I'd want to be a wilderness guide, it seems like kind of a limiting education, but it would be fun. Can we go see it?"

Elise laughed at her daughter's enthusiasm. "Yes, we'll go. Click on the button. We'll set it up."

...

Mary came to the breakfast table smeared in a light gray, sticky substance. Nancy was picking cooked bacon strips from the frying pan to roll in paper towels to drain the fat. Harry was drinking coffee at the kitchen table with the newspaper opened half way. Mary sat next to him and smashed the newspaper to his lap. Startled, Harry jolted in his seat. Mary's nose was now four inches from his own.

"Good morning, Mary," Harry greeted with patience. "What do you have all over you?"

Her flannel night gown was smeared front and back. Her hair was stuck together in sticky tangles.

Nancy turned from the stove to check her mother. "I don't know what this is, unless, maybe, let's see, is it ice cream?"

Abigail entered the kitchen with a yawn.

"Sis, will you check Mom's bed while I start the eggs? She has something all over her gown and in her hair."

"Sure." Abigail took a closer look at their mother. "It might be the chocolate ice cream. Did you check in the freezer?"

"No, she just came in." Nancy opened the freezer and discovered there was no carton of ice cream. "I think you're right. Better go check her bed."

Nancy set the bacon aside and made the family scrambled eggs and toast. Abigail came back to report that Mary had, indeed, taken the ice cream to her bed sometime during the night. It had melted and leaked out of the box making a mess of all the sheets and blankets. "I put them in the laundry. After breakfast, I'll make her bed with fresh ones and wash the dirty ones. You go ahead with your plans to ride today. It's gorgeous out there already. Maybe the weather will hold for your November camp out next weekend."

"Thanks, Sis. Breakfast is ready."

Everyone was seated, and Harry said grace. Without waiting, Mary began eating. She ate bacon with her fingers directly from the serving plate before Harry said, "Amen."

Nancy picked up the platter, gave Mary one more slice, and handed the plate to Harry. Mary reached over and took another handful of bacon. Abigail distracted their mother while Nancy put Mary's extra slices onto her own plate. They quickly passed the platters of eggs and toast to each other before Mary could grab more than her share. They each ate while guarding their plate from Mary.

"How was your date with Larry last night? What was it, your fifth?" Nancy hoped for her sister's sake that Larry Wright would be Mr. Right. She was concerned, however, that if and when that happened, it would leave a void with help caring for their mother.

"Our sixth, but who's counting? He sure is a gentleman. He reminds me of you, Harry."

"I don't know about that." Harry was embarrassed. "I hope he treats you right. You're an exceptional person. You deserve someone who treats you well."

"Thank you. Time will tell, I guess. Speaking of Larry, can we invite him here for Thanksgiving? I'm kind of afraid to ask him." Abigail pointed to Mary with her head.

Harry, always wise, pointed out, "That could be a test of his understanding, patience, acceptance, and degree of caring. I think it would be a good idea."

...

Chapter Five

November Camp Out

Charlie hoped that he would not run into Slade when he arrived at Buckeye Farm. He was not sure how he would explain his presence there. If all went well, Lavern would be there. It was Saturday, and she would not be at the school. *If I see Lavern, well, the rest is up to her. I'll talk to her and see if she's changed her mind about me. We belong together. If she's not willing to see it, well, I'll try to take her back again until she understands we're soul mates. If she's willing to come back to me, I'll forgive her, if not, ...*

Slade would not identify his car as belonging to him, so, as long as he did not run into him directly, he could check around the barn and pasture. Charlie did not find Lavern, but he did run into Bristol, who was unsaddling her horse in the crossties of the barn aisleway.

"Hey, Bristol. How are you? Let me take that for you." Charlie reached for the saddle.

"Thanks, Charlie. I'm good. You?" Without waiting for his answer, Bristol showed Charlie where to place the saddle. "Thanks. Are you looking for Lavern?"

"Yeah. Have you seen her around?"

"Not for a while. I usually come in the daytime during the week, and I guess she comes evenings or weekends. I don't know if she's out riding, or if she moved her horse from here. Lacy and the trailer are both gone."

Charlie looked dejected. "I was hoping, I thought ..."

Bristol looked Charlie in the eye and asked, "You want to get even, or get back together?"

"Yeah. Either or, I guess."

"You have a lot to get even for, Charlie. I mean, she sent you to prison, right? Give me your phone number, and I'll call you if I see her, her horse, or her trailer around here, or if I hear anything." They exchanged numbers, and Charlie left before Slade would find him there.

...

Lavern was indeed out riding her horse. The three friends decided that November was not too cold for a last weekend ride. They returned to Beaver Creek, one of their favorite places. They set up camp on Friday evening just before dark. The time change made it more difficult and they finished with flashlights.

Jolene carried wood to the firepit and laid a fire. She had made fire starters using empty toilet paper rolls stuffed with dryer lint and drizzled with melted candle wax. After lighting a few sheets of newspaper loosely balled up and strategically placed with three of the fire starters, the tinder caught, then the kindling. She tended the fire until the logs blazed, then sat back on her lawn chair to enjoy it. One long stick, two inches around, she reserved as a fire poker. Throughout the evening, she would move the burning logs around to receive more oxygen to create higher flames. She added logs as necessary to keep it going.

Nancy came to the fire wearing a goose down jacket, knit hat, and gloves. She sat down and covered her legs with a throw. "It's good to see you, Jolene. I'm glad you still ride horses with your mother."

"I love to ride! I hope I can always have a horse. It's such a pleasure not only to ride, but to be in the woods. It's so beautiful on trail." She poked a log that had rolled away from the main fire back into position. Sparks flew.

"You know, I heard that if you put copper in a fire, the flames turn colors like blue and green. It would be fun to try sometime. Maybe we could find some copper tubing or something at a hardware store, or maybe your grandfather or your father could scare us up some scrap from one of their construction sites."

"Oh, that would be fun. I'll ask."

Elise joined her daughter and friend at the fire. She wore a heavy Carhart jacket, scarf, and gloves.

Lavern was the last to finish her set up and join the gang at the fire. She was last to arrive at camp because of having a late start after teaching that day.

"Did you bring papers to grade, Lavern? If you brought themes, I'd love to read them. I always get a kick out of them. Remember the assignment to write about baseball? Your student wrote one sentence, 'It rained out.' I couldn't believe you gave him an A! He didn't really do the assignment."

"I gave him the A for creativity and perfect grammar, then told him never to try that stunt again." Lavern laughed at the memory. "But no themes to grade this weekend. I give them a break from Friday theme writing at the end of each grading period. This is the Friday they didn't have to write. It works out to make a better weekend for me."

Nancy mentioned the spelling tests Lavern sometimes brought to grade. She had her students use the spelling words in sentences telling them that it did no good to know how to spell the word if they did not know how to use it. One student had written, "My little brother is omnipotent." The next sentence was, "God is obnoxious." Clearly, he had mixed up the two spelling words.

"What's it like having Bristol at your barn?" Jolene wanted to know.

"I don't run into her a lot. If she goes there, it must be through the week while I'm teaching. The thing is, it seems to me, and I don't want to be paranoid, but it does seem like I'm getting strange looks from some of the other boarders. And some that used to be friendlier don't say hello anymore. Maybe it's my imagination, but I wonder if she's talking badly about me." Lavern rubbed her hands together for warmth then stuck them in her pockets.

"Just because you're paranoid doesn't mean they're not after you," Jolene quipped.

"About being after me. You know Charlie's back. He came to my school asking about me."

The others gasped at this news. Lavern went on. "Since I know he's trying to find me, I talked with Slade about Lacy. We put her in the back pasture with the retired horses, took her name plate off the stall, and made it look like she isn't there anymore."

"What about your trailer?" Nancy asked.

"That's the thing that would be a give-away, so I was going to ask you and Elise if I could park my trailer at one of your homes for the winter. By spring, Charlie should have given up looking around Buckeye Farm for Lacy and me." Lavern glanced back and forth between her two friends.

"Yes, of course," Nancy answered.

"Or you can park it at my house," Elise told her.

"Better at my house," Nancy advised. "The barn is farther back from the road and you could park behind it. He'd never see it driving past, or even coming into the driveway."

They decided that at the end of this weekend on Sunday, Lavern would unload Lacy at Buckeye Farm then bring the trailer over to Nancy's. She could winterize it there and leave it until the first camp out in the spring.

"How safe do you feel personally, Lavern?" Elise asked the question the others had also wondered. "Do you think he would come after you?"

"I don't think so, but I don't know. You would think he had time to cool off by now, and that he wouldn't want to do anything that would land him back in prison." Lavern pulled her blanket more snuggly around her. Thinking about Charlie gave her a chill. "He doesn't know where I live, but he knows I keep Lacy at Buckeye Farm, and he knows where I teach."

"Keep your pepper spray close by all the time," Jolene advised. "And know which way the wind is blowing."

"And check into one of those life alerts, or emergency alert buttons you can wear. You may not have time to take out your pepper spray, but the button would always be with you, around your neck, so you could call for help." They all agreed with Nancy about that.

"How's the college hunt going, Jolene? Have you visited any yet?" Lavern asked, but Nancy was interested, too.

"I have two college visits set up. One is at Hocking Hills Tech to look at their two-year Wilderness Horsemanship program. The other one is at Findlay University for Equine Business

Management. I think that one has more career options. It links equestrian studies with another program like journalism, marketing, computer science, or public relations. I'm leaning toward the computer science. It would be valuable in any career, and personally, too." Jolene repositioned the logs on the fire and added one.

"Yes," her mother agreed. "Findlay combines equine science courses with traditional business administration classes. It would be a broader education." Elise smiled at her daughter. It was hard to believe that her family had once considered abortion. Now here she was, the light of her life, making college plans and choosing a career. Elise reached out for her hand. "I love you so much, Honey, and I'm proud of you. You're such a joy!"

The friends watched the fire for an hour as they talked quietly. Lavern finally called it a night. "Jolene, don't add any more logs to the fire for me. I'm going to have to go to bed." She yawned. She loved her teaching job, but it did tire her. She was a good teacher and put substantial energy into her students. The worry over Charlie also consumed her energy.

The others watched as the flames died to glowing coals. Jolene spread the coals apart and they each went to bed.

The temperature dropped to the low forties over night, but the women stayed warm in their horse trailers with living quarters. With their furnaces running and heavy blankets on their beds, they kept warm. It was cozy for them, but they were reluctant to climb out of bed in the morning.

Nancy made coffee for herself and Elise. Jolene and Lavern slept until nine. Nancy made another pot of coffee and they had a shared breakfast of cooked oatmeal with brown sugar, walnuts, and bananas, plus Elise's pumpkin bread with cream cheese.

Mucking the manure and dropped hay from under the picket lines, hanging new hay bales, and carrying water for the horses warmed them up. With breakfast and chores finished, the group talked and drank coffee as they lingered around the campfire Jolene built.

"What time are we riding?" Jolene asked.

"Whenever. Before or after lunch?" Nancy hoped they would agree on after lunch.

"Let's go right after lunch. It'll be warmest in the afternoon. We could ride until four or four-thirty, then heat up my chili for our supper." The women enjoyed Elise's chili, plus inertia had set in while the fire mesmerized them, and they all agreed to this plan.

By one o'clock, lunches were finished, horses were groomed and saddled, and riders were mounted.

"Which way?" Jolene wanted to ride in the lead.

"The orange trail, starting from the blue trail," Lavern offered.

"That works for me," Nancy chimed in.

Jolene took off on Tricked Out and Tucker placed himself immediately behind his barn buddy.

Elise was worried about crossing Beaver Creek at the half way point. "Jolene, if anyone goes into the water today, it'll be too cold. It could cause hypothermia. We should probably turn around there and come back the same way instead of doing the loop."

"Oh, Mom, you're such a worry wart," but Jolene remembered the time Tricked Out fell in the river with her.

Nancy, who was behind Elise, overheard. "I agree. It's too cold to take a chance. We'll turn around there. It all looks different from the other direction, anyway."

They headed to the main park in Beaver Creek where there were picnic tables, restrooms, and picket lines for the horses. The scenery was stark with bare tree trunks rising above the gray rocks and brown leaf-covered trail. The sun created lacy shadows on the ground through the nearly bare branches. Only dots of yellow and brown leaves still clung to the trees like an impressionist painting. Here and there were patches of ferns, moss covered downed tree trunks, and dark evergreens. Gray clouds covered the sky making the daylight dim. They breathed in the scent of damp earth and leaves and pine deep in the forest of conifers and deciduous trees. It was chilly riding, only in the fifties, but with long underwear and good jackets they were comfortable. The horses moved out smartly in the cool temperature. There were several creek crossings where the water was not as deep as it was at the half way point. The horses splashed through the shallow water making the riders laugh.

The trail led up a lengthy hill then dropped down to a grove of pine trees that led to the main park where they took a break. Back in the saddle, they back-tracked and reached camp four hours after starting out. They were ready to return. Fingers were starting to grow numb with cold and there were still horses to unsaddle, groom, feed, and water before they could eat their own supper.

Around the campfire that evening, they laughed at themselves all bundled up in hats, scarves, heavy jackets, gloves, and wrapped in blankets.

"Make it a small fire, Jolene. I'm not staying out here long. I'm going in and putting the furnace on." Nancy was thinking about cuddling up with a good book under her warm covers.

"Same here. Early night for me. Worrying about Charlie has me exhausted." Lavern wanted to go to bed to sleep.

"Mom?"

"Me, too, Honey. It's a bit too cold for me out here when we have a furnace inside. I'll stay out with you for a little while, but let's go in and play some five-hundred rummy. Bet I can beat you!"

The next day's ride was equally as enjoyable and uneventful. They started out earlier so they could be back in time to break camp and drive home before dark. The damper on their pleasure was knowing that it was the last camp out for the year.

...

Chapter Six

Thanksgiving

Bristol had been fired from her job at the age of sixty-six. She decided to retire instead of hunting for another position. Being retired gave her plenty of time to spend at Buckeye Farm talking with other boarders. She repeated her lie that Lavern cut off Hot Stuff's tail. Sometimes she added a fabrication that Lavern caused her ex-husband to go to prison with false accusations of abuse. Some of the boarders, who did not know Lavern well, believed Bristol. Others, who knew better, decided to keep their distance from Bristol.

Two of the boarders talked over their concerns about Bristol's information, and decided to approach Slade about them.

"We don't want her cutting our horses' manes and tails," they told him.

Slade assured them that they had been listening to rumors that were untrue. *I was afraid that one was trouble when I heard her harping at the blacksmith. Guess I'll have to have a talk with her.*

Slade caught up with Bristol two days later. He spit tobacco juice and cleared his throat. "Bristol, Ma'am. I understand you've been warning my boarders about the possibilities of another boarder cutting their horses' tails off?"

"I sure have! It's that Lavern Smith, or Esser, or something. I used to ride with her and her friends. They cut Hot Stuff's tail then laughed at me when I found it on the ground. You need to keep an eye on her. Better yet, the barn would be better off without her. You don't want to start losing your boarders. She's a nasty piece of work. Did you know that she accused her husband of abuse and got him sent to prison? We don't need someone like her around here."

"Ma'am, I don't know how your view became so slanted, but I've known Miss Lavern for long enough to know none of that is true. I also happen to have heard the real story about the cut tail. It wasn't an entire horse's tail, it wasn't from your horse, and it wasn't Lavern who placed it under your horse as a joke. I guess what that says about you is that you can't take a joke. Now, why you're blaming Miss Lavern for sending her husband to prison is a mystery to me. Were you friends with her then? He tried to kidnap her, he bruised her ribs, he choked her, split her lip, and blackened her eye. He knocked one of her friends down and broke the nose of the forest ranger. I understand that you're leaving all of that out of the rumors you've been spreading about her."

"Well, I, I ..." Bristol, normally quick witted, sputtered.

"No need to say anything. In fact, saying nothing is what I want you to do around here. Say nothing about any of the other boarders. I want no gossip, no rumors, and no boarders who spread it." Slade spit and walked away before the sputtering Bristol could say anything.

Bristol decided that she would leave Slade's barn if that's how he was treating her, but she could not leave while she and Charlie had business with Lavern and her horse. *Charlie! There's an idea. I'll invite him over for Thanksgiving dinner. I won't have to be alone.* Bristol's parents were leaving for a cruise early that Thursday morning with her mother's sister and her husband, Aunt Kay and Uncle Dean. Bristol's sister, Lucy, was spending the holiday with her boyfriend and his family.

...

Charlie decided to try to follow Lavern from her school again. If she had moved the horse from Buckeye Farm, he would not be able to find her there, so this was a better bet.

The Wednesday before Thanksgiving, he parked in the direction she and the other woman headed the last time. The teachers began to trickle out of the building. He used the binoculars and caught Lavern and the other woman walking toward what appeared to be Lavern's truck. *They must ride share, take turns driving.*

He watched as they climbed into the truck, Lavern driving. He threw the binoculars on the seat and started his engine, ready to pull out behind them.

Charlie was able to follow Lavern all the way to an apartment complex which he guessed was where she was living. He had tried to stay two and three cars behind her truck. Now he pulled into a parking lot large enough that his car would not be noticeable. He was ten slots down from Lavern's truck with three vehicles between them. A large building of several units was on each side of the parking lot, with two more buildings next to each of these. The other woman walked to the building across the lot. Lavern entered the building directly in front of her truck. When she disappeared inside, Charlie hopped out.

He ran up to the door and pulled. It did not open. *Locked!* He looked around. No one else was coming. Not wanting to call attention to himself, he went back to his car to wait for an opportunity. It only took twenty minutes when he saw an older lady park close to the same entrance, exit her car, and take two bags of groceries from her trunk.

Charlie hurried over to her. "Here, let me help you with those, young lady." He reached for the bags.

The woman happily handed them over. "Why, thank you, young man, and you are young. I haven't been called young for too many years."

They walked toward the entrance. "I'll get the groceries, you get the door."

The unsuspecting woman unlocked the door and held it open for Charlie.

"Do you want me to take them into your apartment for you?"

"Oh, no, I can manage after you take them up to 215. Even with the elevator, the walk down the hall can be long. Guess I'll have to get me one of those carts that can haul several bags at once."

Charlie was busy looking around for any sign of Lavern's apartment. No names were on the doors, only numbers. A row of mailboxes in the lobby were marked with apartment numbers only.

When they reached 215, Charlie asked, "Can you keep a secret?"

"I guess I can. What kind of a secret?"

"A romantic one." Charlie smiled his best charming smile.

"Oh, I love romance. Yes, still do. What's your secret, young man, and don't tell me your name so I can't forget and tell your secret."

"Shh, but I like the looks of the pretty blond girl who lives in our building here. The one who drives a truck. Do you know her?"

"Oh, Miss Esser has a secret admirer! I love it!"

"Yes, but keep it a secret. Do you know which is her apartment? I want to leave her some flowers from her secret admirer."

"Why, yes, she's up on the third floor somewhere, but I don't know which unit. I'm sure you'll run into her time to time. Take my advice and start a conversation with her. She's a fine young lady. Now, I'll open my door and you can hand me my groceries." She unlocked her door. Charlie handed her the bags. "Good luck, young man, and thank you for your help."

And thank you for yours, Charlie thought. *I'm so close now.*

...

Thanksgiving Day, Marty drove separately to the Parker family home for the afternoon feast. Elise and Jolene would go to the Evans family Thanksgiving get-together with her parents and her brother, Wyatt, in the early evening. Marty seldom joined them there.

Elise had been growing more excited about going to college. She could see only pluses to pursuing her abandoned dream, and could foresee no minuses. All she needed was approval from her husband and her father-in-law. The money for books and tuition, after all, would have to come from them.

During the meal with Marty's parents, brothers, and sisters-in-law, Elise dropped the bomb. She spoke to Devon, Marty's father. "I want to go to college. I still want to be a family lawyer."

There was sudden quiet as all conversations stopped and everyone looked expectantly between Elise and Devon. Jolene's jaw dropped open until she realized it and swallowed her food.

"Do you, now?"

Elise nodded her head yes to answer her father-in-law.

"What brings that on?"

People returned to eating, but all ears were listening to the conversation between Elise and Devon.

"I think looking at college programs with Jolene made me start thinking there isn't any reason why I can't go to school now."

"You're how old?"

"Barely thirty-four." Elise began to sweat. She hoped no one noticed. Everything depended on Parker approval, Devon's and Marty's, especially Devon's.

"And how old would you be when you graduate? Or, more importantly, when you would earn your Juris Doctorate and be eligible to take the bar exam?" Devon had not returned to his food. He did take a sip of water.

"About thirty-nine or forty? I could begin classes this coming semester, and go to summer school." Elise squirmed under Devon's scrutiny.

"I guess you'll be forty someday anyway, whether you go to school or not. You might as well be a lawyer when you're forty. You have pleased me, my dear, over the years. You never complain, and you have given my boy a good home and a beautiful daughter. I know I was originally against this marriage, but it turned out. Yes, it turned out all right."

Devon turned to Marty. "I'll pay for her tuition as long as she has decent grades. You buy the books. Maybe instead of going into family law, she'll come into our family business as counsel." He began eating again.

"Yes, Sir." Marty did not question his father. It was never worth it. Anyway, he had no objection to Elise going to school as long she continued to keep a good house.

"Mom!" Jolene whispered to her. She squeezed her mother's left hand under the table. Mother and daughter smiled at each other. "Just don't choose my school." Elise laughed.

...

Thanksgiving Day, Nancy, Harry, and Abigail had Larry over for the traditional feast. The sisters were busy in the kitchen when Larry arrived. The men talked easily with each other in the living room. Mary was in the bathroom. It was Harry's job to monitor her while Nancy and Abigail prepared the meal.

"Will you excuse me briefly?" he apologized to Larry when Mary was gone too long. "Time to check on my mother-in-law. We're afraid she could hurt herself with some of the things she manages to do."

"Of course. Take your time."

Harry walked down the hall. The bathroom door was open. Mary was dunking the purple puppy in the toilet, up and down, up and down, splashing toilet water throughout the room.

"Mary, what are you doing?" Harry, not wanting to be splashed with the toilet water, stayed outside the door.

"Dirty puppy, dirty puppy. Gets a bath. Gets a bath. Splish splash, splish splash." Mary took the puppy out of the water and twirled him around her head. Water sprayed around the room.

Harry ducked away from the open doorway and groaned. The sisters were going to love this on Thanksgiving Day. He took a deep breath and went to the kitchen to inform them.

"What can I do to move the dinner along while you two clean up your mother and the bathroom?"

Larry, having overheard the problem, volunteered to help. "I'm actually pretty handy in the kitchen."

The sisters gave instructions to the men, and their apologies to Larry, and went to clean up the wet mess. After cleaning the bathroom and their mother, they had to take their own showers again and put on clean clothes. Dinner was ready before they were.

...

Friday after Thanksgiving, Nancy, Lavern, Elise, and Jolene met at the local Cracker Barrel. They tried to meet at least monthly after the camping season ended, beginning with this holiday weekend.

"We were so lucky to have decent enough November weather to camp out one more time," Nancy remarked after saying a short grace before their food was delivered to the table.

Everyone agreed.

"How was everyone's Thanksgiving?" Nancy asked.

They all shared their holiday events. Elise told them she

decided to go to college and her father-in-law agreed to pay her college tuition. Her friends were surprised and happy for her. She told them about her desire to be a family lawyer.

"How about you, Jolene? Do you still write to Randy?" Nancy asked after updating them about Larry and Abigail.

"I do." She smiled a mysterious Mona Lisa smile.

Lavern wanted to know, "Will you and your mother be going to the same school?"

"No!" Elise and Jolene exclaimed simultaneously.

"I'll stay at home and go to Kent State for pre-law. After that, if I pass my LSAT, I'll apply to Akron U for law school. Jolene is going away, and hasn't quite made up her mind where, have you Jolene?"

"No, Mom, not for sure yet, but probably Findlay for their Equine Business Management. Hey, has everyone been riding?"

Only Elise and Jolene had gone on a day ride since the camping trip.

"I have my horse trailer over at Nancy's now. It's winterized. I'm only going to ride around the farm this year," Lavern told them.

"Do you see Bristol much? What does she have to say?" Elise wondered.

"No, not much, and we don't talk at all."

"How is your mother, Nancy?" Lavern inquired.

"She's a handful of trouble. Harry and I think she's getting worse, but Abigail doesn't want to admit it. Did I tell you she's dating a nice man?"

"Your mother?" Jolene quipped.

Everyone laughed. "No, my sister."

The women wanted to hear all about that. Everyone hoped it would work out. "The only thing is, it scares me that with Larry in her life, she's going to want to move to her own place again, and I don't think Harry and I can handle Mom alone at this point. I hate to think of putting her in a home, but even if Sis stays, that time is getting closer."

They made plans for their New Year's Eve party. It was Elise's turn to host. She doubted Marty would stay home for the party. He might pass through and talk with the other men for a few minutes. Randy, Jolene's boyfriend, would come, and Nancy's husband, Harry. They would miss Ric being with them. He was well liked, but since Bristol was no longer part of their group, it would be awkward to invite him.

Their meals came, and the women enjoyed the food, conversation, and each other.

...

Chapter Seven

December

Bristol called Charlie when she noticed Lacy in the far back pasture with the retired horses. "Lavern's trailer isn't here, but Lacy is. Can you come on short notice? I'll call you on a night when no one is around, and you can meet me at the barn. You can get to Lacy, and if Lavern's trailer still isn't here, you can borrow my rig. If her trailer is here, I'll pull it with my truck, if it isn't too far. I'm assuming you'd be taking it to the horse auction in Sugar Creek?"

"That's my plan, yes. Thanks, Bristol." *Unless I can find her first and make her take me back.*

Bristol was gleeful about the trouble she was about to provide for Lavern. She wanted to share her delight, but she was friendless at this time. She called her sister.

"Hey, guess what, Lucy? I ran into Lavern's ex-husband at the barn, and he wants to get even with her by taking her horse to the auction at Sugar Creek. I told him I'd let him use my truck and trailer, and I'll drive him there. Miss High and Mighty is about to get hers!"

"What will happen to the horse at the auction? I mean, who will buy it? Will it go to a good home? How would you know?"

"Probably it would be sold to a meat buyer. Most of them go to slaughter from that auction."

"Why are you doing this, Bristol? Is it to help Charlie get his revenge, or is it to get revenge of your own? What has that poor girl done to deserve losing her horse this way? And isn't it theft? Couldn't you be put in jail for stealing, or helping to steal, her horse? Won't they ask you questions about ownership at the auction?"

"Gee, Lucy, I thought you would support me, not criticize me. You're my sister. Don't you see the beauty in a double revenge with one action?"

"No, Bristol, I don't. I see no beauty in revenge. What does this say about you as a person? Give it a rest. Why don't you try to be more caring about how other people feel?"

"Because they don't care about me! Why are you criticizing me? I don't need that! You're not my mother."

"No, I'm not Mom, and I'm glad I'm not. She has always been negative, especially toward you, but also to me. She puts us down, lies about us to make us look bad, and tries to send us on guilt trips. Why don't you learn from her and be the opposite? Develop a more positive approach to other people? How about showing support to others instead of, of, well, of treating them the way you do?"

"I treat people well when they treat me well."

"How many friends do you have now, Bristol? How is your approach to other people working for you? You need to be able to forgive, to support, to be loyal, to be kind. Try to curb your sarcastic tongue. We were raised in a church, so act like it. Remember the Golden Rule? Do unto others the way you would have them do onto you? Or that one about turning the other cheek?"

"I'll turn the other cheek! I'll show them my bottom cheeks. Anyway, who are you to tell me how to be? I'm doing just fine. Do you think you're some perfect person? Get out of my life!" Bristol hung up in anger.

...

The Christmas holiday was approaching, and Lavern's goal was to teach a unit on punctuation before her students left on the twelve-day break. Many of them would forget the lessons if she gave the final test after they returned.

She faced her classroom of students. "Your Friday themes show me most of you need work on correct punctuation. Tomorrow we will begin a punctuation unit. As always, we will start with a pre-test. If you already know how to use punctuation correctly, you will not have to do the work in class or the homework. I will put all A's on the pretest into the grade book. If you receive a B on the pretest, you do have to do the work in class, but not the homework. Everyone else will do class work and homework, of course. So, no homework tonight, unless you want to study the next chapter in your books to prepare for tomorrow's pretest."

After teaching a unit, Lavern would give her students a check test. Those with an A on the pretest would not have to retest. Usually there were only one or two students who had an A on a pretest. Anyone with an A on the check test would have that A entered in the grade book, and would not have to take the final test. There were always several students who earned an A at that point. The day after taking the check test, Lavern would hand out the corrected test papers. She would arrange their desks in groups so each group had at least one A and B test grade student who could help the others. She passed out classwork for her students to work on in their small groups, hoping the A and B students could get through to the others where her own teaching had not. Homework that night would be for any student without an A in the gradebook for that unit. The next day, they would grade their own homework as she explained the answers, then she would pass out the final test. Whatever grade they earned would be entered into the grade book.

Lavern always took it to heart when any one of her students failed a unit grade. She constantly critiqued her teaching style to see if she could reach every student.

This morning, Eileen Brumbridge and Lavern had driven to the school separately. Lavern needed to run a few errands before going home. Approaching her truck after school, she kept peering around to make sure Charlie was not there. She did not see him because he was parked near the front of her apartment building, waiting for her to arrive home, and hoping to catch her.

When he observed Eileen parking her car and Lavern was not with her, he waited another hour before giving up and driving off. Shortly after, Lavern came home. Unaware Charlie had been there, but worried he may have somehow figured out where she lived, she took out her pepper spray before unlocking her truck. She looked around before opening the truck door, then looked around again when she climbed out. She hurried to the apartment door with her briefcase and gave a sigh of relief as it closed and locked behind her. She hated living this way. Would she ever feel safe again?

...

A horse barn is always a draw for wild animals like raccoons, and opossums. They eat the grain dropped by the horses as they chew, or the undigested grain in the horse manure. Neither Elise nor Jolene would poison the wild animals. When they saw signs of a wild one in the barn, they placed a piece of apple in a Havahart trap, trapped it live, and took it over five miles away to set it free in an unpopulated area. They understood the local law called these wild animals vermin, and they were supposed to be destroyed if trapped, but neither of them could bear to kill them. Over the years, they had trapped ten raccoons and five opossums.

The first snow of the season came the first week in December. A light dusting fell the first day. Leaves and tufts of grass stuck up through the glittering white crystals. The second day, the snow barely covered the grass. On the third day, there was enough snow to reveal footprints and tracks.

Elise fed and watered the horses each morning as soon as Jolene left for school. Jolene did the barn chores in the evenings after supper. This morning on the way to the barn, Elise saw typical bird tracks, two prongs forward, one longer prong back. It looked like two or three deer had wondered across the lawn and along the pasture fence. Another set of tracks led directly into the barn. Half those prints had four toes in front of what looked like a miniature baby's footprint with a dot in front of each of the toes. The other half had five toes, each with a dot in front, and what looked like a partial tiny palm print behind.

The light switch was right inside the barn door. Elise slid the door open and reached in to turn on the light. She saw a beautiful black and white skunk blinking in the sudden brightness. She stood still and watched it lumber out where enough of a depression had eroded in the dirt so it could slip under the back barn door.

With a sigh of relief, she entered the barn.

"Pretty kitty, you can have an apple for a snack. It's trap time for you," she thought out loud as she went about caring for the horses and setting the trap. *And what do you do after you trap a skunk? But we can't let it hang out here to possibly squirt us some time.*

Elise no longer bothered to inform the uninterested Marty about anything having to do with the barn or horse management, and she forgot to mention the skunk to Jolene. After dinner that evening, Jolene went to the barn to do the chores. She shortly came running back to the house crying, "Mom, Mom! You set the trap and caught a skunk! There's a skunk in the trap! What are we supposed to do now?"

Elise laughed. Marty, who was in the living room, looked up from the newspaper he was reading and frowned. "Not *my* problem. You figure it out."

Elise put on her coat, hat, gloves, and barn boots. "Come on, I'll go out with you. We can do this without being sprayed." She grabbed a small tarp she had brought from the basement earlier in the day and they trudged through the cold to the barn.

The skunk was scrunched up inside the Havahart in the center of the aisle. "Poor thing. He must be so scared. I'll go in. You stay here in case he sprays before I can cover him."

"Mom, do you really think he won't spray if you cover him with a tarp?" Jolene waited right outside the door.

"I think he can't spray if he can't stand on his head, and he has no room inside the trap to do that. I'm covering him just in case."

With the tarp over the trap, Elise carried it to the open bed of the pickup truck and returned to the barn. "I'll help you with the barn chores, then you come with me to let the skunk go."

"OK, but I don't know about this."

They drove the skunk to the nearby state park where they intended to let it go in the woods where it belonged. It was seven PM and fully dark. The park road had few street lamps. No other cars approached from the other direction. Then Elise saw headlights shining into her rearview mirror from behind. Suddenly she was afraid for their safety. Who else would be in the park on a winter night? She checked to be sure the doors were locked and the truck had at least a half tank of gas.

"We have company, Jolene. If that car bumps into us, I'm going to keep driving. No matter what happens, don't get out, and keep the door locked. I've heard of men smashing into the rear end of a woman's car, then raping her when she gets out to see the damage. Look, there's a road to the left up there. I'll turn, and we'll see what he does. Hopefully he'll continue on straight."

The other vehicle followed them through the turn.

At the next cross street Elise turned right.

"Mom, it's a park ranger behind us." Jolene saw the light bar on the top of the vehicle from the glow of one of the rare street lamps on the corner as they made the turn.

The park ranger turned, too. He no doubt wondered what they were doing in the park after dark in the winter. Elise hoped he would not stop them to find out, and ask her what was under the tarp. She knew it was illegal to free the skunk in the park, but she could not kill it, and she did not want to free it where it could be a nuisance to others.

"Now what, Mom?"

"We'll drive out of the park and hope he doesn't stop us and see the trapped skunk in back."

She made another turn, the ranger right behind them. The next turn took them out of the park. "OK, we made it. I guess we'll have to take this guy back home again. Maybe this experience will make him afraid to ever come back to our barn."

At home, Elise pointed the trap door toward the pasture, away from the barn. She stood behind the trap, reached over the top of it, gently rolled the tarp away from the door, and opened it carefully. The skunk did not move. She was not sure which way the business end of the skunk was pointed. It was all black and white hair against the wires of the cage. Was it too scared to move, or did it not see the open door? She tipped the trap and gently rocked it. The skunk came out and lumbered away toward the fence.

"Well, that was something," Jolene said from behind her mother where she was hiding from the skunk. "I hope we don't trap it again. I hope it stays away, and all its family, too."

Mother and daughter looked at each other and simultaneously burst out laughing, thinking about the skunk and the park ranger. They laughed at themselves laughing so hard. They grew weak in the knees, then weak in the legs, and dropped to the ground now laughing uncontrollably at themselves for lying on their backs in the snow unable to quit laughing. Finally, they were able to stop. As they lay recovering their breath, Jolene began to make a snow angel, moving her arms and legs for the wings and the gown. Elise watched then made her own snow angel. Jolene jumped up and offered her hand to her mother. They stood there with their arms around each other, regarding the pair of angels in the snow. They walked back to the house, still linked.

...

Nancy and Abigail finished putting dinner on the table and called to Harry and Mary to come eat. Harry came in from the living room. Mary was missing. Her coat was still in the house.

"I'll check the basement," Harry volunteered.

"I'll go upstairs and look." Not yet worried, Abigail climbed the stairs.

Nancy put the serving dishes of food in the oven on warm, wiped her hands on her apron, and began looking around in odd places. Mary was not in the coat closet. She was not behind the shower curtain in the bathroom, or under her bed or in her closet. One easy chair in the living room was far enough from the wall that Mary could hide behind it. She was not there. Nancy joined Harry in the basement to help search in all the possible places there.

They searched for fifteen minutes before deciding Mary must have left the house. Harry had installed locks on the front and back doors higher than Mary could reach to keep her safely inside when she came to live with them. "I just checked the locks, and I must not have latched the back door lock when I came in from the barn," Nancy told her sister and husband. "She must have gone out, but she doesn't have her coat." It was thirty-eight degrees with a prediction of dropping to twenty-five overnight. It was too cold to be outside without winter clothing.

"We'll find her," Harry reassured the sisters. "Sis, you go next door to the Phinney's, then over to the other side to the Lohman's. Maybe she went visiting, although I'm surprised they wouldn't have called us. Nancy, take the truck and drive west down the road. I'll take my car and go east."

They all hurried into their coats and gloves. "Everyone take your cell phone," Nancy instructed.

"Right. If we haven't found her in twenty minutes, I think we better call the police for help searching. We have to find her before she gets hypothermia from exposure." As a retired hospital nurse, Abigail knew what that could mean.

"Sis, if no one has found her in twenty minutes, you come back home and call 9-1-1 then wait for the police. Nancy and I will continue searching with the vehicles."

Everyone left on their assignments. Nancy called Elise and Lavern on her cell phone as she drove. Both of them joined the search.

Half an hour later, no Mary. Abigail had a frustrating time with the police dispatcher who kept telling her she could file a missing person's report in forty-eight hours. She finally made the dispatcher understand their mother had Alzheimer's and could not legitimately be somewhere safe. They needed help to search in the cold before it was too late.

It was a knuckle biting forty-five minutes before two officers showed up at the door. Abigail let them in. Harry, Nancy, Elise and Lavern were still driving around searching.

She did not offer them a seat because she wanted them to go out to search.

"Mind if we sit down? We have a few questions that will help us in the search."

Abigail sighed and pointed to the sofa. She sat on the edge of one of the two chairs and answered all their basic questions.

"OK, we'll search for a while here, and if she doesn't turn up within a couple of hours, we'll call for volunteers. Where does she usually go? Where do you typically find her?"

"She likes to go to Walmart, but it's way too far. She couldn't possibly walk that far, and I doubt she would know what direction it's in anymore, anyway, which means if she's walking there, she could be on any road."

"What about here on the property? Do you have any out buildings? Garage? Shed? Barn? Anything unlocked that she could enter?" The officer glanced up from his notes.

"The barn! I don't think anyone checked the barn!" Abigail put her arms back into her coat and flew out the door without taking the time to zip it or to put on her boots. She raced to the barn in back, her shoes becoming wet with snow. The officers were right behind her.

She slid open the barn door, stepped inside the dark barn, and switched on the light. Bright Beauty looked up from chewing her hay. On the other side of her was Mary, hugging Beauty's neck.

"I don't have carrots. Did you bring carrots? The horse wants carrots."

"Oh, Mom! You had us so worried. Aren't you cold?" Abigail opened the stall door and tried to lead her mother out. "Let's get you in the house and warmed up."

"I want carrots! The horse wants carrots! Did you bring carrots?"

"Come on, Mom. The carrots are in the house. Let's go get them." Abigail knew by the time they reached the house, Mary would have forgotten about the carrots and the horse. She turned to the officers. "Thank you for coming. I don't know why we didn't think about the barn. We were just so worried, we were frazzled."

One officer reported to dispatch that Mary had been found. When they reached the house, Abigail called her Nancy and Harry, who were jubilant at the news. Nancy called Elise and Lavern. Everyone was relieved at the happy ending.

...

Chapter Eight

Holidays

Bristol had been invited to Christmas dinner with her daughter and her family. Ric had been invited, too, so Bristol decided not to go. She was curious about him, but she did not feel like putting up with the awkwardness. She called Charlie to see if he wanted to come over for a turkey sandwich on Christmas day. She was not about to cook a meal. She had not put up a tree. Why bother? She had bought no presents. She was angry with her sister and her mother, and decided not to see them. Charlie declined her invitation, so Bristol spent Christmas alone.

New Year's Eve for Bristol was just another night. Who wanted to go out when everything was so much more expensive? Who cared about a ball dropping? She would not miss sleep over such a silly thing.

...

Lavern spent her Christmas day with Nancy, Harry, and Abigail. She was able to help out with the dinner prep and with keeping a watch on Mary. Abigail's friend Larry joined them. It was a cheerful, pleasant gathering. Lavern was pleased Harry would be coming with Nancy to the New Year's Eve party at Elise's. He contributed much to the conversations and the fun.

...

Elise was in a holiday mood. She and Jolene celebrated Christmas in their traditional way with Marty and his Parker family until two in the afternoon. It was always formal, and a little stiff, but lovely. For Elise, the fun began when she and Jolene left the Parkers to go to her own Evans family gathering. Wyatt was always a little loud, teasing, joking, entertaining. Feeling warm and joyful from her family Christmas gathering, she was delighted to plan the New Year's Eve party for her friends at her house.

The Christmas tree remained up, and she added a Happy New Year banner to the decorations. It was pot luck. Elise made a vegetable and cheese tray, Swedish meatballs, and punch with floating, melting ice cream. She set a beautiful buffet table and played soft music in the background. She asked Marty if he would stay and interact with her friends, at least for a little while.

"They're your friends, not mine," was his answer.

"They could be your friends, too. We do things with husbands now and then. Harry will be here with Nancy, and Randy is coming to be with Jolene. It would be enjoyable for them to have another man around. Ric won't be here because Bristol isn't in our group anymore. I guess they divorced, anyway."

Marty did his usual pass through, although he stayed twice as long, however short, talking with Harry, who drew him in for twenty minutes.

After dinner, Randy turned the music up. He showed Jolene two new dance moves. Lavern tried them out, too. Randy grabbed Elise by her hand and had her dancing. Harry and Nancy watched with delighted amusement.

They ended the evening playing games Elise had prepared. The most fun was the drawing game when your team had to guess what you were drawing, similar to charades. They laughed at each other to the point of tears.

Two minutes before midnight, Elise poured sparkling grape juice into wine glasses and handed them out for the New Year's toast. The ball came down, Randy and Jolene kissed, Harry and Nancy kissed, everyone hugged everyone else, and the toasting began. Elise wondered where Marty was.

...

Chapter Nine

January

The winter weather had so far stayed milder than usual with highs ranging from thirty to forty-five degrees. Charlie had thought he might catch Lavern at Buckeye Farm while the schools were on Christmas break. The New Year holiday had come and gone with no sign of Lavern at the farm or while he sat in his car watching her apartment. He had limited time to watch because of his job. He had been hoping to catch her before the cold snap predicted three days from now. He had wanted to give her one more chance to take him back before Bristol called, but she never showed up while he was watching and waiting. So, when Bristol called to say no one else was around the barn and he should come right away, he agreed. It was time for revenge.

Charlie parked at the far end of the lot, away from the barn. It was after dark, perfect for their clandestine operation. He called Bristol. "Are you here? I'm outside."

"Yeah, come on in the barn. No one else is here, and guess what, Lacy's in a stall. We won't have to go to the back pasture for her. Come on."

Bristol opened the stall door, haltered Lacy, and attached the lead rope. She led the mare out of the stall, and Charlie slid the stall door closed again. He followed Bristol, who was leading the horse, down the long barn aisle.

Bristol stepped outside to take Lacy to her trailer and nearly bumped into Slade.

"What are you doing with someone else's horse?" he asked before spitting tobacco juice. "Hey, this is Lacy, Lavern's horse. Why do you have her? Where are you going with her?" Slade reached out and took the lead rope out of Bristol's hand. He turned the horse around to lead her back to her stall and saw Charlie lurking inside the barn trying not to be seen.

"And you! What are you doing here? Up to no good, both of you. Get out, and get out now. If I ever see either of you here again, I'll call the sheriff. I've a good mind to call the sheriff now and report you for horse stealing."

Bristol found her voice and spoke up with what she hoped sounded like authority. "We were helping Lavern out. She's a friend. She asked us to walk her horse for her each evening when she couldn't make it to the barn, you know, to keep its joints loose." It did not sound believable to anyone.

"I know that isn't true. I know you aren't friends with Lavern, not the way you talk about her behind her back. Besides, if her horse needed anything, Lavern would have discussed it with me. And Charlie, I know who you are, a man with revenge on his mind when your trouble was of your own making. Bristol, if I ever see you again, it better be to watch you load your own horse into your own trailer to take her to some other barn. In the meantime, do not ever come back here, or you either, Charlie."

Bristol started to give Slade some lip, but Slade cut her off. "Be glad I haven't called the sheriff on you tonight. Now get lost, both of you."

Slade stood in the barn doorway watching as Bristol and Charlie left in their vehicles. He walked Lacy to her stall. In spite of what he told the would-be culprits, he called the sheriff. He wanted the attempted theft on record. His next call was to Lavern to let her know.

"So, you need to stop by the sheriff's office to fill out a restraining order for your apartment, your school, and the barn."

"But he doesn't know where I live, as far as I know. I thought about a restraining order before, but my address would have to be on it. I'm afraid for him to have it."

"Well, Missy, why don't you drop by the sheriff's office and talk over the pros and cons with them, yeah? I told Bristol to move her horse out of here and not to come back until the day she moves him. I wish I had my shotgun with me when I saw that Charlie skulking in my barn. He wouldn't be sitting down for a while. I'm half inclined to give Bristol a load of buckshot in her arse, too."

...

Spring semester began in January. Elise was registered for three classes. She wanted to start out easy until she was back in the groove of studying. She planned on continuing through the summer with another course or two. She hoped it would not interfere with her summer riding, but her priority had to be on her education. She finally had her chance to become what she had always wanted to be. She was not about to blow it now. Besides, she needed to set a good example for Jolene.

Pre-law was a minor. She chose psychology for her major. She felt it would be helpful in family law.

The classes held her interest, and so did the attentiveness of another nontraditional student, a good-looking man about her age who wanted to be a criminal lawyer. His name was Cody Cash. He sat next to her in two of her classes, one by assignment, one by his choice.

"Hi! Good morning," he told her breathlessly as he slid into his seat. "I saw you walking along campus, and I hurried to catch up, but you were too far ahead. It's good to see you." He smiled looking directly into her eyes, his head tilted slightly.

"Oh, good morning to you. I would have waited for you had I known you were behind me."

His eyebrows shot up and he grinned. "Would you, now?" He smoothed back his long, dark hair.

Elise smiled. "Did you read the section for today's class?"

"Yes, I read it. Did you?" Without waiting for her answer, his nostrils flared slightly, he leaned toward her and quietly commented, "I found it interesting." *She sure smell good. Fresh and clean.*

The professor walked in and began class. Cody kept his body turned toward her as much as he could while sitting in a seat beside her. Now and then he leaned in and whispered something to her about a statement the professor made. When she made a comment in class, he whispered near her ear, "That was astute."

After their first class, he walked with her to their next one. When that class ended, she remained in the room for her last class. He had to go to another building. He picked up his books and gently touched her arm as he left. "See you Wednesday."

A week before their first test, he asked her to exchange phone numbers. "Maybe we can get together to study."

Elise hesitated. *Am I playing with fire? I'm enjoying him too much. It wouldn't hurt to study together, but I'll have to draw the line there.* She gave him her cell phone number.

...

Abigail woke Harry who was sleeping lightly in the recliner in the living room. "Go to bed with your wife. It's my shift. Is Mom in bed?"

"She went to her room fifteen minutes ago. She wandered through the house the whole time until then."

Mary was wandering all night most nights. Nancy, Harry, and Abigail had to take shifts throughout each night to keep a watch on her. They were lucky to be able to doze for a few minutes in the recliner during their shift. None of them was sleeping enough.

Mary would move things around. She would hide objects in bizarre places. Nancy found Mary stuffing money from Abigail's wallet into the tea kettle. They finally found the wallet in the freezer.

They had to install locks on the kitchen cupboard doors and chain the refrigerator doors closed. Day and night, Mary would try to cook and was a potential threat to starting a fire. She would also try to eat foods raw that needed to be cooked. Potatoes, meat, pasta, cake mixes, had all been tried raw.

There was constantly something new and disturbing Mary would attempt, and the family would have to stop her.

Harry went to bed with Nancy. Abigail opened Mary's bedroom door. Mary was not in her bed. Abigail stepped inside the room. The closest door was open. Only a few of Mary's clothes were left on hangers. The rest had been pulled to the closet floor and Mary lay on top of them, sleeping. Abigail left her mother there and went to the recliner. She hoped to doze for a few minutes before Mary would be up to wander.

Mary's home in Ravenna had been sold and the money transferred to her bank account. The insurance company for her long-term care plan had been contacted. The doctor's form had been filled out and faxed in. The insurance company agreed to activate payments when Mary was placed in a home. The time had come, even though Nancy and Abigail had desperately tried to keep their mother home. They had narrowed their search to two homes. They hoped to make a decision this week.

Abigail forced the issue when she announced she wanted to move into an apartment of her own again. She liked the active senior building where Larry lived. They had a game room, an indoor swimming pool, and an activity director who planned many programs for the lively seniors as part of their rent.

Watching over Mary to keep her and the household safe was difficult for the three of them. When Abigail moved out, it would be impossible for the two of them. Nancy was crushed, but she understood it was necessary. She prayed God would lead them to the best placement for Mary to be well cared for and happy.

...

Chapter Ten

February

Bristol moved her horse to a new barn on fifty acres with trails through woods, around hay fields, and around the perimeter of the property. Bristol was anxious to try the trails. She bundled up against the cold.

Hot Stuff was close to sixteen hands high. Bristol was on the short side and normally had difficulty mounting. Today she could barely bend her legs because of the extra clothing. She carried a mounting block to her horse, stepped up, placed her left foot in the stirrup, and swung her right leg over the saddle. She plopped down, air whooshing out of her goose down pants. Hot Stuff snorted and side stepped.

The sun peaked from behind light gray clouds. There was a light breeze, but not a freezing wind. The air temperature was twenty-nine degrees. Bristol was almost comfortable with wool socks, thermal underwear, hat, scarf, and gloves. It would be even better when she rode in the woods with the trees blocking some of the wind.

She had not been riding since the weather turned cold. Hot Stuff was full of energy. He jogged instead of moving in a flat foot walk. He snorted and tossed his head. He skittered sideways as a rabbit crossed their path. Steam blew from his flared nostrils.

They entered the woods. Hot Stuff continued to prance and dance. His long, winter hair became damp with sweat. A flock of wild turkeys rose up from their right side, and he shied to the left before moving on down the trail.

When three deer popped out of the thicket on their right and ran across the trail three feet in front of them, it was all the wired-up horse could handle. He whirled and began a wild gallop along the icy trail back to the barn. Bristol gasped and tried to pull him up. He stretched his neck and kept running. The trail made a sharp right turn. Hot Stuff turned at full gallop. Bristol went flying through the air. Her head and shoulder hit a tree. Her shoulder slid down the trunk. Bones at the bottom of her leg snapped when she hit the ground. She landed on the ground with her back against the tree, her arm over her head, blood dripping from a compound fracture in her wrist. She blacked out.

Half an hour later Bristol came to. She was cold. She could barely breathe because taking a breath caused too much pain. She tried to adjust her position on the cold ground, but it hurt to move. She knew she was in trouble. She had been riding alone. Where was her horse? Did it run back to the barn? If it did, was anyone there to notice? How long until help might arrive? How long had it been?

...

It was becoming uncomfortably cold to sit in the car with no heat. Charlie poured coffee into the cap of his thermos and took a few sips. He rubbed his hands together for friction heat and put his gloves back on. He was sitting in front of Lavern's apartment building watching for her to return home, or for someone to enter so he could follow them in.

A woman and four young children began streaming out of the door. Charlie jumped out of his car and hurried over. He caught the door just as the last one, a boy who looked five or six, waddled out bundled up in his winter clothes, hurrying to catch up to his siblings.

Charlie slipped inside and took the stairs to the third floor. There were ten apartments on each side of the long hallway. Lavern lived in one of these twenty units. Which one? He walked the length of the hall twice with no clue. He should have planned better.

He left the building to drive around searching for a florist shop. *Hey, a grocery store. Don't they sell flowers?*

They did, and he bought two small bouquets. Together they were full and colorful.

Back at the apartment building, he did not have to wait as long to enter. On the third floor, Charlie rapped on the door in the middle of the hallway. No one answered. He tried the next door. An older man in a sleeveless white undershirt, the waist of his sweatpants riding under his large belly, answered.

"Yeah? Whad ya want?" he asked with a cigarette wagging between his lips above a three-day growth of beard. "I ain't buyin' nothin'." He eyed the flowers suspiciously.

"Oh, no, Sir, I have a floral delivery for a Lavern Sm…, uh, Esser, but there's no apartment number. Do you know her? Which is her apartment?"

"She's the school teacher three doors down this side, always helpin' out. Brought me homemade chicken soup when she knew I was sick and I got no missus." He scratched his chest. "Whoever sent um, she deserves um. She's a right good girl." He closed the door.

Charlie knocked on 316. No answer. He was not surprised because her truck was not parked out front. Still, he thought he would try. He waited in the hallway for an hour for her to return before giving up. *There's always another day. At least now I know exactly where she lives.*

...

Cody Cash was smitten. He was infatuated with everything about Elise. He liked her girl-next-door looks, her hair, her natural make-up, her delicate perfume, the way she walked, the way she talked, what she had to say, her laugh, her insights, her gentleness, her femininity. She was friendly and seemed to like him, too, but she also seemed closed off somehow. He could not figure her out.

They had been meeting an hour before their first class to study together. They each prepared questions to quiz the other. It was working well for them as a review. If a test was scheduled, they met two hours early. That meant an early morning for Elise, but it was worth it to do well on the tests. If she were honest with herself, it was worth it to spend additional time with Cody.

Ten minutes before class began, they would take a break. Cody answered her questions about himself readily, but she was reticent about sharing her own personal information. Sensing she was not ready, he was too polite to push.

Six weeks later, he decided to take a risk. When their study session ended, he reached over and brushed an eyelash off her cheek. In his deep, masculine voice he murmured, "You know I'm interested in you, don't you, that I want to do more than be your study partner? Tell me what's holding you back." He reached for her hand.

She did not pull her hand away, but she looked down and was silent, trying to gather her thoughts. Yes, she had been playing with fire.

"If you don't think we have enough time now to go into it, how about you give me your address and I'll pick you up for dinner tonight. You can take all evening to tell me over a bottle of wine." He waited.

Finally, she spoke. "Cody, I like you, too, truly I do, and I would love to see what could blossom between us. What I haven't told you is, I'm married."

Cody jerked his hand from hers as though it was a hot potato. Elise's heart fell.

"Wait. My marriage is a sham, a marriage of convenience. There was never any love. I never had any love."

"Go on," he said stiffly.

"We married because I was pregnant. I was pregnant because I was a naïve sixteen-year-old who thought he cared about me. He never did. We have always lived separate lives. My daughter and I are well provided for, but that's all. I have never been loved or made to feel relevant except by my family and friends. You are a new experience for me."

"So, I'm just an experience, or an experiment." Cody was gruff, disgusted.

"No, no, that's not what I mean. Please don't put words in my mouth. I enjoy being around you enormously. I look forward to seeing you. I relish the time with you. I don't want what little we can enjoy to end, but I can't have more."

"Because you're married."

"Because I'm married."

"I never saw that coming." He stood, picked up his coat and books, and walked out the door. He did not stay for class that day.

Elise may as well have not stayed, either. She was not able to concentrate. She was heart sick. *Play with fire and risk being burned. I was willing to risk it for myself, but I should have thought about what it might do to him.*

...

Harry helped Nancy and Abigail move their mother into the locked Alzheimer's unit in the assisted living facility they had chosen. The private rooms were clustered around an enclosed outdoor courtyard where the patients were safe to wander. The staff ratio was one to three, night and day. An activity director with a staff that included a music therapist planned several activities each day. The menu was varied and nutritious, and the food the family sampled was delicious.

Nancy and Abigail looked crestfallen as they sat in the conference room waiting for the administrator to finish the paper work checking Mary in. Harry put an arm around each of them and tried to console them. "You are more upset than she will be. You know she doesn't remember anymore. She won't be longing for her house in Ravenna, or her home with us. She hardly knows us anymore. This will be a new reality without reference to a past. She lives in the moment. Cheer up." He gave them each a pat on the shoulder.

The administrator agreed with Harry. "Your mother will probably be content here. We make every effort for the comfort, safety, and enjoyment of our patients. You're welcome to come visit anytime you want."

"I'm not upset," Abigail admitted. "I feel relieved. We deserve to have our own lives. We can't keep Mom safe at home anymore, and we're wearing ourselves out. This way, we can have more energy, visit Mom often, and enjoy our time with her."

...

Chapter Eleven

Desperate Measures

Bristol lay moaning on the ground. How much time had passed? It was still daylight. When would help arrive? Would help come? She could not move without pain. Her shallow breathing was painful. She would never be able to stand up and walk out.

What's that? Someone shouting?

Yes, people were shouting from back along the trail toward the barn. They were shouting her name, but she could not respond. She did not have enough breath. *Hurry, hurry, I need help. I need oxygen. I can't breathe.* Bristol closed her eyes. When she opened them, she saw two women she did not know from her barn on the trail before the bend.

"There she is!" one woman in a red coat pointed and they both ran to her.

"Looks like you need help," Blue Coat said.

"I'm calling it in to 9-1-1." Red Coat held her cell phone to her ear. The dispatcher asked questions. In turn, Red Coat asked Bristol and relayed her answers.

It was another hour until the paramedics arrived on the trail pushing a stretcher loaded with medical equipment and supplies. They asked her questions until she begged for oxygen. They slipped the oxygen mask over her head and started an IV line after cutting her jacket.

"That's an expensive goose down jacket," she complained.

"You want some pain killer, don't you? You're going to feel better after we start this morphine drip."

Bristol moaned in response. Before she began to feel better, they lifted her onto a back board and onto the stretcher. The jostling was excruciating. She blacked out before reaching the ambulance. She woke up in the hospital.

Someone was asking her questions. The only one that got through to her was, "Is there anyone we could call for you?"

No one. I have no one in my life.

"Bristol? Who can we call for you?" The voice was so distant.

No one. Bristol went back into her narcotic induced sleep.

...

Lavern, dressed comfortably in blue jeans and a sweatshirt, was grading papers when Charlie knocked. She peered through the peep hole. She saw no person, only a glorious display of colorful flowers. *Who? What?* She opened the door, and Charlie pushed his way inside, closing the door and knocking her against the sliding coat closet door. The flowers dropped to the floor in a riot of color.

"What? Charlie! What are you doing here?" Lavern tried not to let her fear show. He was standing inches from her, arms outstretched, his palms leaning on the closet door, one on each side of her head, pining her to the door. She was terrified.

"Finally, Darlin'. It's been awhile. I've been searching for you ever since I've been out." He stared down at her lips.

Lavern was afraid he was going to kiss her, or worse. She tried for casual as though a welcome friend had stopped in.

"Come in the living room, Charlie. I'm sorry you've had a rough time, really, I am. Come in and sit down. Would you like a cup of coffee? I remember how you drink it." She tried to duck under his arm, but he kept her pinned.

"What I want is for you and me to make a baby and be a family. Remember, I told you family means everything to me. You said family means everything to you, too, but you left me. How could you leave me? How could you send me to prison?" Charlie hit the sliding door with his fist. The thin wood cracked.

"Look what you made me do!" Charlie yelled.

"Charlie, I didn't do anything but stand here and listen to you. Come on, let me make coffee." Lavern's voice quavered.

"You haven't changed, have you Lavern? You're still arguing with me. You should have learned by now not to argue with your man."

Charlie's hot breath was moist against Lavern's face as he stood over her. She wanted to remind him he was no longer her man, but he would only become angrier, possibly to the point of physical violence.

"I, I ..." Lavern couldn't think of what to say as she concentrated on slowly moving her hand toward her chest where her emergency call button hung from a cord around her neck. Charlie was searching her face and not observing her hands. If she could just touch the middle of the button without his noticing her gradual movement, she could call for help.

"Say you want me back. We could be the way we were before. Just get rid of that horse so we can be together, do everything together. I have my job back. I make good money. You can quit teaching and be a homemaker, have babies. We'll make a family. We can buy a house, if you want."

Lavern felt the call button. Her index finger moved toward its center. She pressed.

"Emergency Call Service," the voice announced through her device. "Can we be of assistance?"

Charlie jumped back. Shocked, he looked down and gaped at the pendant Lavern wore.

"Send police! I have an intruder!" Lavern yelled to make sure she could be heard.

Charlie yanked the pendant, forcefully. The cord broke. The voice continued. "We have your location as 2056 Youngblood, Building C, Apartment 316. Is this correct?"

Before Lavern could answer, Charlie threw the pendant on the floor and stomped on it, smashing it. It was silent.

Lavern ran. Charlie blocked the door to the building hallway that was her only exit. She was trapped inside the apartment. She made a dash toward the bathroom hoping to lock herself in, but Charlie was quicker. He grabbed the back of her shirt and pulled. She lost her footing and fell. He lost his grip on her shirt when she rolled. She scrambled on her hands and knees and shot up right as he reached down to grab her again. He caught one leg and pulled. She belly-slammed the floor, violently.

Charlie stood over her, panting. She lay still, catching her breath.

"Why are you doing this?" he asked her, confused. "I thought you loved me. I thought we were a family."

She rolled over on her back and looked up at him. "We were, Charlie, until you began to mistreat me. You need to move on, now. I'm not yours anymore."

Charlie dove on top of her, pinning her to the floor with his body. Her left hand was free. She groped for the top of the coffee table next to her, feeling for the glass candy dish. There! She gripped it securely and brought it down on Charlie's head as hard as she could.

She pulled her arm back to take a second swing, but Charlie grabbed her wrist and bent it back. The candy dish dropped. A bone snapped. She screamed in pain.

"Now look what you made me do, Lavern. You shouldn't have called me an intruder. You shouldn't have tried to get away."

"You're right, Charlie. You're always right. Will you take me to the hospital now? My wrist is broken. You will do that for me, won't you?"

Charlie sat up to look at her wrist. She clutched her left arm to her chest in an attempt to protect the injury.

Sirens sounded in the distance, coming closer.

Charlie reached down and pulled Lavern to her feet. She screamed in pain. He shoved her toward the sliding balcony door. "Open it! Hurry!"

"I only have one hand, Charlie." She fumbled with the latch one-handed. Fearing his intention, she stalled for time. The sirens were closer.

Charlie reached past her, slid the door open, and pushed her out. He intended to throw her over the balcony. "If you don't want me, then no one else can have you. I couldn't live with that."

The sirens were loud, close. He shoved her toward the edge. The barrier was waist high. Adrenaline coursed through her. She screamed in fear. She fought to keep herself away from the edge, but it was a small balcony. Charlie had her bent backward over the barrier as the police cars rolled to a stop in the parking lot in front of the building. With her good right hand, Lavern clung to the railing. She wrapped her legs tightly around Charlie's torso, gripping with all her strength to keep him from tossing her over.

"Back away from the balcony!" a policeman shouted up at Charlie. "Step away from the woman!"

Charlie looked down to see four officers with guns trained on him. *They won't shoot me while I'm this close to her. I'll toss her over and run.* But Charlie could not free Lavern from her adrenaline-powered life and death hand grip on the railing or her legs from around his body.

They struggled together. One of the policemen tried to enter the building to gain access to the apartment, but the heavy outside door was locked. A second policeman ran to the end of the building where he also faced a locked door. The two remaining officers kept their guns trained on Charlie. If it looked like Charlie was going to lift Lavern over the railing, they would have to take the chance and shoot.

"We have the building surrounded. You can't get away. Step away from the woman or we'll shoot."

Charlie could not have stepped away from Lavern if he had wanted to, her legs were wrapped around him in such a death grip. He would pry one of her legs free, and when he started to pry her hand loose, she would grab his body with her leg again. Finally, he struck her left, broken wrist. She screamed and dropped to the balcony floor. Before he could reach down to pick her up and throw her over, two shots rang out. Both hit their mark. Charlie's skull exploded, pink mist and brain matter splattered.

Lavern, hysterical, screamed and screamed. By the time the police had the building manager unlock her apartment door, an ambulance had arrived. Lavern had no voice left. She had crawled to the farthest corner of the balcony and curled into a fetal position. She was rushed to the hospital. The police would have to question her later.

...

Elise called Marty at work while Jolene was in school. "You need to come home. We have to talk."

"Can't it wait? What could be so critical I have to leave work?"

"Look, Marty. I know you don't care that much, if at all, about your family, but this concerns you. We need to talk before Jolene comes home. I've never before asked you to leave work, so you must realize this is important, and I'm not willing to tell you over the phone."

Marty sighed. "All right. Give me an hour to finish up and drive home. This better be worth it. I have projects to finish."

Marty marched into the house, put out. He found Elise in the living room with the gas fireplace turned on, a lap blanket across her knees. She was thinking about the intense, emotional conversation to come, choosing the right words, deciding how to explain.

"Come and sit down," she called out.

"What's this about? If you make it snappy, I can get back to work and not ruin the whole day."

"It's kind of about what you just said, I mean your attitude, your attitude toward me and even toward Jolene, that we don't count, that we aren't important."

Marty frowned and glared at her.

"We seem like such an inconvenience to you. Jolene started asking questions about our relationship. She believes, as I do, that you don't love her, either."

"So, you called me home from work to say that? You knew I didn't love you when I had to marry you." Marty was incredulous.

"Well, it's a starting point. I always hoped love would grow between us. It hasn't. I don't love you, either, Marty. I don't know where you go during all the time you aren't home with me, and frankly, I don't much care. The point is, we don't love each other, we lead separate lives, and I'm lonely for a caring relationship, for real love."

"You want me to care more," Marty stated flatly.

"It would certainly be nice if you did, but, no, I'm not asking for that. I'm telling you, although you provide well for us, you aren't giving me the emotional love and support I need. I found someone who can."

"What!?" Marty jumped up from the chair and paced the room. "You met someone at school? How long has that been going on?" Marty was shocked. He never viewed Elise as someone who could be desirable to someone else.

"Yes, I met someone who gives me the attention I crave, treats me like I matter, and actually talks with me and cares about what I think. The details I'm not going to share with you. I never ask you where you're going, where you've been, or who you've been with. However, I'm telling you this much because I don't want to go behind your back. You are my husband, by law, anyway."

"Are you saying you want a divorce, or permission to have an affair?" Marty wiped his hand across his forehead and sat back down.

"I don't know what I want, but I don't want to be dishonest. You don't touch me at all anymore. When you did, it wasn't with love. I'm tired of being lonely. I mean, I have Jolene and my friends, thank God, but I'm lonely for a real, caring, love that makes me feel I'm important and valuable. When Jolene goes off to college, it will be even worse for me. I need to explore this relationship for the promise it shows." *It may be too late, but if I'm going to pursue it, I'm going to do it honestly.*

Marty was stunned.

They sat speechless for a few minutes. Then Marty stood. "I'll get back to you." He left the house.

...

Nancy hummed a cheery tune as she walked from the parking lot to the Alzheimer's unit to visit her mother. She was thrilled because her mother had settled in to her new home immediately and seemed to enjoy it there. The staff was friendly and attentive, the food good, the activities plentiful. It was a blessing for the rest of the family to have their lives back and Mary safe and content.

"Hello, Mom. How are you doing today? Did you have a good breakfast?"

Mary looked at her blankly. She and other residents held a styrofoam noodle kids used in swimming pools. They were using them to keep a balloon aloft. As the balloon came toward them, they would bat it away. Mary used hers to slap the top of Nancy's head.

It did not hurt, but Nancy gently took her mother's hand and told her, "No, Mom, don't hit other people. Try to hit the balloon when it comes." Nancy helped her mother play the game. Several of the other patients had aides helping them.

The activity ended in fifteen minutes. A music program began. Some of the patients clapped hands in time to the music, some swayed in their seats, some stood and danced in place. Mary danced her purple puppy on her lap.

A nurse wheeled a cart into the activity room and dispensed pre-lunch meds to some of the patients. A patient began banging on a table, off beat. An aide redirected him. An activities staffer handed Nancy the next month's schedule. "Thought you might want to have this." Nancy thanked her. The music program ended and an aide announced it was time for lunch.

Mary cried enthusiastically, "Food! Eat! Food! Food time!" She gleefully took Nancy's hand and began walking to the dining room. Nancy smiled to see her mother so eager. *We should have brought her here long ago.*

...

Chapter Twelve

Hospital Visits

Bristol had several broken ribs, a trimalleolar fracture (three broken bones at the bottom of her right leg), and a compound fracture of the radial head (the wrist end of the long bone in her arm). She lay in her hospital bed with no one to care. She felt isolated and alone. There had been so many friends over the years, friends she rejected or who rejected her. *Why? Why? What did I do? Why am I so disliked?* She thought back to high school. There was no one she could call from there. She thought back to her jobs at the boutique and the accounting firm. No, she had no friends from there. She thought about the various clubs she had joined and left or been asked to leave. No friends, no one. Her family? Her mother lied about her, belitted her, and did not protect her against Uncle Dean's molestation. Her sister thought she was mean and was mad at her. Ric left her, and she was never close with her daughter. *Aunt Kay? I'll call Aunt Kay.*

"Hello, Aunt Kay? I fell off my horse and I'm in the hospital."

"I'm so sorry, Bristol. Are you seriously hurt? I guess not, you're talking with me. I'll let your mother know. She'll want to come to see you. I'll hang up now and call her."

"No, don't call Mom," Bristol implored a dial tone.

When her mother found the time to call her, hours later, she sniffled and choked as though she were crying. "My poor daughter! I'm so distraught! I want so desperately to see you, but

I have to stay home to care for your father. He takes more of my time now, you know. I feel terrible! Oh, my! My poor baby! It pains me so much not to see you. I'm going to call my friends to ask them to pray for you." Elizabeth hung up.

Bristol knew her mother would call her friends crying and sniffling how awful she felt that her daughter was hurt, then not bother to visit. It was only about herself, not about Bristol, the old Poor Me game.

No, I have no one to call, no one to care.

...

Lavern did have loved ones to call. She called Slade, then Nancy. She briefly told each of them what happened, that she was in the hospital because Charlie had attacked her and broken her wrist which now needed surgery. She told them the police shot Charlie and killed him. She broke down in tears each time she talked about it. She was going to call Elise next, but Nancy volunteered to inform Elise for her so Lavern would not have to repeat the terrifying news.

Within an hour, Slade was sitting by Lavern's bedside holding her good hand, encouraging her to drink water, fussing with her covers to keep her warm, asking if she needed anything, until Lavern fell asleep. He watched her sleep until Nancy and Elise came in.

"Shh," he whispered tilting his head toward Lavern. There were only two visitor chairs in the room. Slade rose, offered his chair to Elise, and pulled the other chair closer to the bed for Nancy.

They quietly introduced themselves to Slade.

"What do you know? Has she told you anything?" Nancy asked.

"They're doing surgery on her wrist later today. Charlie came into her apartment. I'm not sure yet how he got in. She pushed her emergency button. He tried to throw her over her balcony. The police came when they were out there on the balcony, and they shot him in the head. Killed him instantly. The whole thing was traumatic for her. She's sedated."

"Yeah, that's all she was able to tell me, too," Nancy whispered.

Elise was still astonished. "Wow, we were right to worry about him for her. I'm glad we encouraged her to get that emergency button."

Nancy was concerned about Charlie. "I should have been praying for Charlie to overcome his jealousy and control issues and find true love in his heart. I wish I had prayed for him as much as for Lavern. I'm afraid he died without salvation."

Lavern opened her eyes. She murmured.

"What, Honey, what can we do?" Elise leaned over to hear better.

Lavern did not answer. She reached for her friend's hand and smiled.

Slade handed Lavern's water to Nancy. Nancy held the straw to Lavern's lips. She took a few swallows. "You all came. You're all so precious." She closed her eyes, and they immediately flew open. "No!" she shouted in a raspy voice. "Every time I close my eyes, I see Charlie's head being blown apart, again and again." She began to cry.

"It's PTSD, Honey," Slade explained. "It will take some time to heal emotionally as well as physically. Don't let him win this last round."

"That's right," Elise agreed. "Think only about the positive. You are forever safe from Charlie. No more being afraid."

"I can't go back there. I don't want to step foot in that apartment again." Silent tears fell down Lavern's cheeks.

Nancy had a plan. "I've been thinking about that. I figured you wouldn't want to stay there with the traumatic memories. I told you how Sis has been dating Larry? Well, she wants to move out for some privacy. We can pick up her furniture from your apartment while you're still in the hospital and move it to her new place. We already moved Mom to an Alzheimer's unit. So that leaves two bedrooms at my house. You can use either one for as long as you want until you find another place and buy your own furniture. How does that sound?"

Lavern cried again and nodded in agreement.

Elise asked how Mary was doing.

"She's content, so we are all happy. She seems to be thriving there with all the attention and all the programs. We should have looked into this for her before. I had no idea it would be a good thing." Nancy smiled. Then her cell phone rang and wiped the smile from her lips.

Before answering she announced, puzzled, "It's Bristol!"

"Hello?"

"You did? How bad?"

"I'm sorry to hear that. Where are you now?"

"Funny, that's where I am, too, visiting a friend."

"Yes, I can come. What room?"

"OK, give me a little time to finish my visit here. See you then." Nancy hung up and told the group about Bristol's accident. "She's right down the hall. I guess I'll stop by before going home."

Her friends frowned. "Don't worry. I don't intend to rekindle a friendship with her, only dispense a little comfort and a prayer for healing. Speaking of which, can we hold hands around Lavern's bed and pray for her peace, comfort, and rapid healing?"

Slade joined the circle. Nancy prayed. Lavern thanked them and smiled.

...

Nancy walked into Bristol's hospital room. She had no idea what to expect. *Why did she call me? What does she want? It's been so long.*

"Bristol, are you awake?" Nancy whispered.

Bristol opened her eyes. She pushed the button to raise the head of her bed. "Yes, I'm awake. Sit down."

"What happened?"

Bristol told Nancy how she came off Hot Stuff at a full gallop and broke ribs, arm and leg. She ended with, "No one has come to see me. I'm all alone."

"What about your mother, father, sister?"

"My father isn't up to going out anymore. My mother uses him as an excuse not to come. My sister's mad at me. My daughter, I don't know, she doesn't care. I don't have any friends."

"Why is that, Bristol? Have you given it any thought?" Nancy used a gentle tone that she hoped was not judgmental.

"I'm all alone."

"I understand that, but why is it, do you suppose? You seem to go through friends frequently. Is that your choice, or theirs?"

"Sometimes I drop them when they can't, when they aren't, when they don't …"

"That's all right. You don't have to tell me. It's for you to figure out for yourself, but I suspect you drop them when there is nothing in the relationship for you, when they no longer can do anything for you. And other times?"

"They get mad at me and don't want me around anymore. People can be such jerks."

"You perceive them as jerks when they become mad at you, but do you have any idea why they are mad at you? How they perceive you? What causes them to see you that way?"

Bristol looked blankly at Nancy.

"OK, Bristol. What makes a good friend?"

"Someone who likes what you like and can help you."

"Then, have you been a good friend, helping them? Tell

me about the times you have helped your friends."

"I have."

"Yes, I know you have. You came to my barn when Bright Beauty had colic that time. When are other times you helped? Are you more of a taker, a user, or are you more of a giver?"

Bristol looked away.

"You say a good friend helps. Have you been a good friend, helping, or are you looking for people who can help you? These are vital questions, Bristol. It seems like you'll be laid up awhile with time to think them over. Your best bet is to be honest with yourself."

"My own mother hasn't come to visit me. I'm not good enough. I've never been good enough."

"Your mother makes you feel like you're not good enough?"

"Always. Always has. I've never been good enough for her."

"She says things that put you down? Insult you? Criticize?"

"All the time. She says I should be more like my sister."

"Do you believe her? What she says?"

"Sometimes. Sometimes I just get mad. It always hurts."

"So, you know how it hurts to have someone criticize and insult you. Are you careful not to do that to others?"

"People can be such jerks. They can be so stupid."

"And you tell them."

"Yes, of course."

"And that makes them feel good and makes them stop being what you think is stupid? Or does it make them feel bad and you feel good?"

"Well, I..."

"Think about it, Bristol. Think about the Golden Rule, 'Do unto others the way you would have them do unto you.' Do you live by that? Do you treat others the way you want to be treated, or do you treat them the way your mother has treated you? How do you make others feel?"

Bristol did not answer.

Nancy put her coat on and stood over Bristol's bed. "I'm going to say a prayer for your healing, physical and emotional. Please think over this conversation. Call me if you want to discuss it more." Nancy touched Bristol's good hand, offered a short prayer, and left.

...

Elise no sooner came home from the hospital than her phone rang. It was Marty. She was surprised. Since the day she had told him she was interested in someone else, she had not seen him. He came home late and left early before she awoke. It had been three days.

"I'm in the hospital, Elise." Marty groaned. "They think I have kidney stones." He groaned again. "They're admitting me. Oh, it hurts!"

"I'll be right there!"

Elise grabbed the coat she had just hung up and her purse, and rushed back to the hospital. Marty was still in emergency waiting to be taken to a regular room. Elise slid into a chair beside him.

Marty opened his eyes. "I've never felt so much pain. I thought I'd die and didn't care if I did. They put some good pain killer in this IV drip. It's better now than it was, but it hurts." He groaned.

Elise was surprised Marty had called her, and she was even more surprised he was sharing so much with her. This was a first. He had always remained private and aloof from her.

"I'm so sorry, Marty. Are they sure it's from kidney stones?"

"Yeah, I guess so. They did an ultrasound. They want to wait to see if I pass them. If not, they'll blast them with some kind of shock waves."

The nurse who came in to check on his IV drip explained, "It's shock wave lithotripsy, or SWL. It causes the stones to fragment into tiny pieces that can be passed in the urine stream. Feeling better?" she asked the patient.

"Some," Marty managed through gritted teeth.

An orderly arrived to move Marty to a room. "He'll be in room seven twelve."

Elise grabbed a cup of coffee while waiting for the nurses to settle him in his room. She called Jolene who would be home from school by now.

"Hi, Honey. I wanted to let you know why I'm not home. Your father is trying to pass kidney stones and he's in the hospital. I'm here with him. I don't know how long I'll be. If you get hungry, there's that left over roast beef in the frig. Make yourself a sandwich."

The nurses gave her the OK, and Elise pulled up a chair beside her husband's bed.

Marty reached out his hand to her. She was confused. *Does he want me to hold his hand?* Tentatively, she took his hand in hers. He squeezed and held it.

"You've always been there for me. Like now, you came for me. You've always been there for me even though I've never been there for you. I'm truly sorry. I took you for granted because I thought you were a burden, someone thrust on me who would weigh me down in my life, keep me from having fun. You didn't, not really. You allowed me to live my separate life. You never questioned me, never complained, never argued. I was a young kid with thoughts of fast cars, plenty of pretty women, and nights on the town, not a wife and a baby.

"I was too young, stupid, and resentful to see how you enhanced my life in ways I never gave a thought to, just took for granted. You've been a good homemaker, but I figured you did that for yourself and Jolene. These past few days I've been looking back and seeing how you've tried to please me even though I've largely ignored you. I always have clean clothes in my closet. You cook every night and make my favorites. You even cook ahead for me when you and Jolene go away on your trips. You've always tried to include me in her life even though I never wanted it. My family can be tough, but you made the effort to always be pleasant. It must have been uncomfortable for you to be around them, especially at first, but you always came to family events. You always did the things that a wife would be expected to do, and I never appreciated that, and I never did the things a husband would be expected to do." Marty groaned.

Elise squeezed his hand. Silent tears ran down her cheeks. "We don't have to talk now, Marty. You're hurting too much."

"No, I have to tell you these things now. I thought I might die with this pain. I don't want to miss my chance to tell you. You forced me to see you in a whole new light when you told me there could be someone else. I don't want there to be anyone else. I want you to stay with me."

"Oh, Marty!" Elise did not know whether it was too late. "I don't know what to say."

"Say nothing, then, not yet. Let me prove to you I mean what I'm telling you. Give me a chance. I'm older now, wiser, and ready to enjoy being a settled, married man. If I had been single all these years and was now going to search for a wife, I would be looking for someone who is like you; loyal, gracious, cordial, kind, considerate, accommodating, and, yes, smart." Marty groaned again.

"My, that's a lot of adjectives! I never knew you thought about me in those terms."

"I didn't know either, not until you forced me to really see you, not until I was close to losing you, and close to dying. Elise, I don't want to lose you. Please help me become the man you want, the man you deserve to have. What do you want from me? What do you need?"

"I want love and passion, closeness and caring, honesty and respect. I want to be cherished. I don't know whether you can give me all of those things."

"Let me show you. Please let me show you. Everything will be different, I promise. Elise, will you be my wife? I mean, will you take me as your husband, a real husband, a husband that *wants* you to be his wife?"

"Marty, we'll talk about this when you're better. You have a lot of drugs in you now."

"No, it's not the drugs talking. I've given this a great deal of thought over the last three days."

"Shh. Go to sleep."

...

Chapter Thirteen

Resolutions

It was difficult for Bristol to see herself in the wrong. Recuperating in the hospital bed, then in the rehab center, she had nothing to do but reflect on Nancy's words. She had the utmost respect for Nancy, her wisdom, and her honesty. She finally had to admit the truth in what Nancy told her. She insulted others when they rubbed her the wrong way, the way her mother insulted her. She manipulated others, the way her mother manipulated people to get what she wanted. She lied about others when it helped her to manipulate a situation, or to exact revenge. She was going to have to try to live her life through the filter of the Golden Rule. But why? Why change? How would she get what she wanted in life? How would she get revenge?

Bristol called Nancy and asked her to come for another visit.

"Yes, of course. Is there anything I can bring you?"

"No. I need to talk."

...

The day after surgery on her left wrist, Lavern went to live with Nancy and Harry until she could mend body and spirit. Harry and Larry moved Abigail's furniture from Lavern's apartment into Abigail's new apartment. Nancy gathered Lavern's clothing, toiletries, and school papers to bring to her. Before her next rent was due, they would box up the rest of Lavern's belongings to store in their barn so Lavern would not have to return to the apartment.

Elise stopped by the Reynolds' home to visit Lavern, then she rode with Nancy to Lavern's apartment and drove Lavern's truck back to the Reynolds'.

Lavern returned to her classroom a week after Charlie's confrontation and death. "I need to focus on my students and teaching instead of on Charlie."

Spending time with Lacy also helped Lavern. She was not riding while her wrist mended, but she enjoyed relaxing while grooming her horse. Slade would stop by and talk with her a little during each of her visits to the barn.

Lavern was thankful for each of her friends, her teaching career, and her horse.

...

Marty passed the kidney stones without further treatment. Elise brought him home. She wondered how their relationship would change. Certainly, it could not stay the same after their disclosures to each other.

Elise settled Marty onto the sofa in the living room and ignited the gas fireplace. She covered him with a blanket and fluffed a pillow behind his head.

"Why have you always taken care of me when I never treated you like I cared?" Marty gazed at his wife with wonder.

"Duty, Marty, duty. It's my duty to provide you with a well-run household and with comfort care like good meals and ministrations when you're sick. Don't delude yourself it's been because of love."

"No, no, I don't. But do you think love could grow between us? I think it could if we both want that. I know what kind of person you are, your good qualities. Maybe I already love you in some ways. I want us to go to Europe for the summer, like an extended honeymoon. We never had a honeymoon. Let's take time to focus on each other, build a strong relationship, fall in love. Let me show you I can be the man you desire. Elise?"

She was skeptical. "Summer school begins in May. I'm planning to go."

"Just this one summer, Elise, please? This is a critical time for us. We need time to focus on each other with no distractions. Europe can be romantic. Come with me. Please?"

Elise was thinking she did not want to feel trapped in Europe, away from her family and friends, if Marty had not changed. On the other hand, if Marty were sincere, an extended honeymoon would allow their new relationship to grow. She felt that God would want her to try.

"OK, but I hold onto my own passport. I want to be able to come back home if we don't get along. I don't want you to park me somewhere and take off on your own for hours the way you do here. If we go, we go to be together."

Marty reached for Elise's hand. He brought the back of her hand to his lips and kissed it.

...

Nancy went to the rehab facility to speak with Bristol

again. She found her reflective, but not repentant.

"Bristol, this will only work if you want to change for the sake of others, not because it will do something for you. Do you want to live by the Golden Rule so you no longer hurt others the way your mother hurts you? Or are you trying to change to have more friends? The idea is to be kind to others for their sake, and a by-product of that is people will like you better. If you curb your tongue only so people like you better, it won't last. You need a true transformation in your heart to start caring about how you make others feel. Try to think of others first instead of your own wants and needs. If you can't say something nice, don't say anything at all. Filter what comes out of your brain before it comes out of your mouth. Speak only words of support, kindness, encouragement. Lift others up instead of putting them down. And do it for their sake, not your own. Become a caring person."

Nancy prayed her words would find their mark in Bristol's heart. She was hopeful because Bristol did not make any sarcastic comebacks. In fact, Bristol, uncharacteristically, listened without comment. Nancy returned home. Elise was going to be stopping there to visit with Nancy and Lavern.

Nancy told her two friends about her talks with Bristol. She asked them to visit Bristol and give her a chance to apologize. "Her current situation makes her a desperate woman. Desperate situations call for desperate measures. She's all alone and has nothing to do but think things over. Maybe now she can understand she's been causing her own misery all her life because of the way she treats others, and she's desperate enough to be willing to transform into a kinder person. My hope is she changes because she realizes she's been hurting others and not because she wants more friends for herself."

"Oh, I think she's realized all along how she's hurt others, but she's never cared. She has tunnel vision thinking she makes herself look good, and she has to hurt back when she thinks someone has disrespected her. She manipulates people into situations that benefit her without caring what it does to them. Selfish, that's what she is." Lavern was adamant.

"Nevertheless, I believe she may be ready to change. We need to support her in that. Let's visit and model unconditional love."

When neither of her friends wanted to see Bristol, Nancy reminded them, "We must forgive others to be forgiven. Come on. We'll go together."

...

Later that week, Nancy, Lavern, and Elise dropped by Bristol's rehab together. Bristol, in a wheelchair, led them down the hallway to a conversation nook where they could sit comfortably. Lavern and Elise were uncomfortable anyway, being around Bristol. She made them feel like a puppy facing a rolled-up newspaper because she was either angry and sarcastic, or calm and condescending.

"Thank you for coming to see me," Bristol told the group. "I actually didn't expect it. Nancy told me about Charlie coming after you, Lavern. I'm sorry that happened to you." Bristol stopped short of admitting she had been helping Charlie to have his revenge against Lavern.

Lavern already knew from Slade that Bristol attempted to help Charlie take her horse. "What were you and Charlie going to do with Lacy the night Slade stopped you? Do you understand the two of you were committing a felony stealing my horse?" Lavern leaned forward as she asked, intent on the answer.

"That depends on the value of the horse. It's only a misdemeanor if it isn't all that valuable. Anyway, who says we were going to take it anywhere?"

"Bristol," Nancy warned softly. She had been talking to Bristol about being honest and about asking for forgiveness. Here was an opportunity Bristol might be passing up.

"Well, I only told Charlie I would help him by loaning him my trailer. Whatever he needed it for was, well, whatever." Bristol refused to look at any of the others. She stared at her hands in her lap. "But, Lavern, I am truly sorry for the trouble you had with Charlie. It must have been scary when he came to your apartment." This was a huge step for Bristol.

"And tried to throw her over her third-floor balcony!" Elise reminded.

"You said you're sorry, Bristol. Are you asking for forgiveness for your part in it?" Nancy pushed.

"I don't need forgiveness. I didn't do anything."

The others looked at Bristol. No one spoke a word until finally, Bristol admitted, "Yes. I'm sorry Lavern. I was causing trouble for you. Will you forgive me?"

"Yes, I will, Bristol. It's all over now. And will you forgive me for anything I might have said or done to make you feel so hateful toward me? I never meant to hurt you."

"Well, yes. OK, so we have a clean slate now?"

"Yes, in a way, but it will take a while for me to trust you again. I hope you can understand that. I don't mean it in a mean way, just letting you know trust is earned." Lavern was thinking she did not want to become friends with Bristol again, so Bristol would never have the opportunity to regain any trust with her.

Elise piped up. "For me, the worst thing I have to forgive you for is the way you spoke to my daughter, calling her stupid and so on. It still grates on me, but I can say I'm sorry for anything I might have done or said to cause you anger, resentment, or hurt feelings."

"She was old enough to know better." Bristol might be trying to do better, but old habits die hard.

Before Elise could respond, Nancy murmured, "Bristol!"

"Well, OK, I shouldn't have said all I did to that poor child that day in Harrison, but …"

"Bristol!" Nancy hissed. "Don't deceive yourself into believing there was justification in your actions and words."

"All right! I'm sorry I yelled at everyone. The joke was not funny to me. I thought you were all laughing at me."

"I'm sorry it was so upsetting to you, Bristol. I don't think the ones initiating the joke meant you to be hurt, but I'm sorry you were. Will you forgive us all?" Elise asked.

"Yes." Bristol was surprised her visitors were asking for her forgiveness. She thought they came only to hear her apologize and ask them for their forgiveness.

"Then you went home and called Charlie to tell him where I was," Lavern stated quietly. "Do you realize what happened because of that?"

Bristol shook her head no.

Lavern continued, "He knocked Nancy down and hurt her, he hurt me, he broke the ranger's nose, and he ended up in jail."

Bristol was unable to accept blame. "That's because of what he himself did, not because of what I did."

"But if you hadn't told him where I was..."

"He would have found you somewhere else the way he did this time, so don't try to pin it on me."

Nancy attempted to keep the conversation on a positive track. "We can all agree what Charlie did was Charlie's own fault. Do you feel sorry you tipped him off, telling him where Lavern was on that camping trip?" She was hoping Bristol would say she was sorry or ask for forgiveness.

Instead, Bristol changed the subject to the recent situation with Charlie. "You guys probably think I told him where Lavern is living now, but I didn't even know myself. I did not tell him. I couldn't."

"I don't want to talk about Charlie anymore. He's gone. I'm OK. I'm free." Lavern was concerned she might have another nightmare about Charlie trying to throw her over the balcony and his brain exploding, if they continued talking about him.

Nancy reminded them, "It's a good first step to forgive each other. Then remember to ask God to forgive you. You know, the Lord's Prayer, 'Forgive me my trespasses as I forgive those who trespassed against me.'"

Bristol was only too happy to change the subject to a more comfortable one. "Your mother is doing well in the Alzheimer's unit then, huh, Nancy?"

"She is. We visit frequently. Sometimes she knows us,

she doesn't, but she seems content. They give good care there, keep her safe, and we have our own lives back. It had become unsafe for us to keep her at home, and very stressful. Elise, tell your good news."

"Marty and I are going to Europe for the summer. We never had a honeymoon. This will be our honeymoon. We'll be gone for ten weeks."

Everyone exclaimed with excitement for Elise. Elise thought to add the news about Jolene's college choice and her own return to school to study law, but her two friends already knew, and she did not wish to share the information with Bristol.

The small group talked for another few minutes. When the physical therapist came for Bristol, they said good-bye and left.

On the way out, Nancy told them it was good to see Bristol trying to become a kinder person, more thoughtful of others. "We need to keep praying for God to help her."

"Yeah, it's a big project," Lavern acknowledged.

"Sure is," Elise agreed.

...

Epilogue

Bristol continued to make progress toward becoming kind and honest. Nancy invited her on day rides with the friends again, but they did not invite her on their weekend camping trips. Enough was enough, and a whole weekend was too much. When Bristol would slip and say something sarcastic, instead of ignoring it, they would tell her, "Be nice!"

Lavern stayed with Nancy and Harry until Slade offered her a bedroom with the run of his house, rent free, if she would do the housekeeping and the cooking. With Buckeye Farm as her permanent address, she applied to the Last Chance Corral to adopt one of their rescue foals. Slade helped her raise and train it. Under his tutelage she became an excellent horse trainer.

A few years later, Slade decided to retire to Arizona to live near his son. He sold the horse farm to Lavern. She could afford it with the money she had been saving, her teaching salary, and the income the farm generated from the boarders.

When Jolene graduated from Findlay University after studying Equine Business Management and computer science, Lavern asked her to move into the now remodeled farm house with her, run the boarding facility as barn manager, and help her start a horse training business. Jolene was thrilled at the prospect. She lived with Lavern until she married Randy, who was now a veterinarian. Lavern sold them enough land with frontage to build a vet clinic and a home behind it. Devon Parker provided the construction of both, giving the newlyweds a head start on their lives. They only needed to supply the clinic and furnish their new home. Marty lent them the money interest free.

Elise went to Europe with Marty with trepidation, fearing it would not work out. Her anxiety was needless. Away from the normal distractions of life, they discovered each other and developed a new relationship. She missed her daughter, and she missed most of the camping season with the horses, but she gained the life partner she had always wanted. Marty was attentive, interested in her, respectful, and even romantic. When they returned home, he did not revert to his old ways. Elise was no longer lonely for a devoted partner to share life and love with. They developed mutual passion, tenderness, and caring. During Jolene's visits back home, Marty enjoyed conversations and discussions with his daughter. He discovered he was proud of both his daughter and his wife.

Elise finished her undergraduate studies, passed her LSAT, entered law school, and graduated with her Juris Doctor degree. She passed the bar exam on her first attempt. After several job interviews, she was hired into a firm where she became the family lawyer she had wanted to be. She found the work as fulfilling as she had imagined.

Nancy, Harry, Abigail, and sometimes Larry made regular visits to see Mary in the Alzheimer's unit. Mary remained well cared for and content living there. Abigail and Larry were enjoying their companionable and caring relationship. Nancy remained the spiritual leader in her group of friends. She was aware of her good fortune having a loving, supportive husband, a dear sister, good friends, faith in God, and forgiveness for her sins. She was happy knowing each of her loved ones believed in Jesus and had asked Him for forgiveness.

...

Discussion Questions

1. Why do you think people listen to gossip without questioning the motivation behind it?

2. Who is your spiritual leader? Are you a spiritual leader for someone else?

3. Is there anyone you need to pray for and bless instead of thinking unkindly toward?

4. When you speak to others, do your comments build them up, give them confidence, guide them positively, support them?

5. Have you told Jesus Christ you believe in Him and asked Him to forgive you of your sins? "Dear Jesus, I believe you accepted suffering on the cross to pay for my sins and give me eternal life, and I ask forgiveness for all my wrongdoings. Thank you, Jesus, for loving me that much. Amen."

ABOUT THE AUTHOR

Janet earned her B.A. in Education from the University of Akron in Ohio. She has loved horses her whole life. She lives on a five acre horse farm with the love of her life, Jack, and their border collie Bailey. Janet enjoys scrapbooking photos she takes while riding and horse camping.

She can be reached at:
JanetRFox_Author@mail.com
And on Facebook As
Janet R Fox Author